The Bobbsey Twins at Cedar Camp

by Laura Lee Hope

This book is a product of its time and does not reflect the same values as it would if it were written today. Parents might wish to discuss with their children how views on race have changed before allowing them to read this classic work.

Wilder Publications, LLC.
PO Box 3005
Radford VA 24143-3005

ISBN 10: 1-61720-471-4
ISBN 13: 978-1-61720-471-5

The Bobbsey Twins at
Cedar Camp

Table of Contents:

Freddie's Surprise

Very still and quiet it was in the home of the Bobbsey twins. There was hardly a sound—that is, of course, except that made by four figures tiptoeing around through the halls and different rooms.

"Hush!" suddenly exclaimed Bert Bobbsey.

"Hush!" echoed his sister Nan.

They were two of the twins.

Again came the shuffling noise made by tiptoeing feet on the front stairs.

"Quiet now, Flossie and Freddie!" whispered Bert. "Go easy, and don't make a racket!"

He turned toward Nan, who was carrying something in a paper that rattled because of its stiffness.

"Can't you be quieter?" asked Bert.

"It isn't me—it's this paper," Nan answered. "I should have taken some of the tissue kind."

"I wish you had," Bert went on. "But it's too late now. We're almost there. As soon as we get everything hidden it will be all right."

Suddenly there was a sound behind Bert and Nan as though someone were choking. It was followed by a smothered laugh.

"What's that?" asked Bert in a sharp whisper. "Do you want to have everybody in the house down here seeing what we're doing? Who did that?"

He spoke a bit sharply, in a tense whisper, but his voice was not really cross. It was as though Bert were the leader of some secret band of soldiers or of Indians, and wanted the men to do just as he had told them.

"Who did that?" he asked again.

"I—I guess I did," answered the voice of his little sister Flossie.

"What did you do?" asked Nan. "You must try to be quiet, dear, else our fun will be spoiled. Better take sister's hand."

"Holdin' your hand won't do any good," answered Flossie, and though she tried to talk in a whisper it was rather a loud one. "Your hand can't stop makin' me sneeze," Flossie went on. "Can it?"

"Oh, did you sneeze, dear?" asked Nan, who, since she and Bert were "growing up," felt that she must take a little more motherly care of Flossie.

"Yes, I did sneeze," Flossie answered. "An' maybe I'll sneeze more again. I feel so, anyhow."

"Don't you dare!" exclaimed Bert.

"She didn't sneeze! Not a reg'lar sneeze!" declared Freddie, who was carrying a cigar box. Did I mention that Freddie and Flossie were the other pair of Bobbsey twins? I meant to, anyhow.

"If she didn't sneeze, what did she do?" asked Nan.

"I did sneeze!" insisted Flossie.

"You did not!" asserted Freddie. "You—"

"Hush! Hush!" cautioned Bert. "You'll spoil everything!"

But Freddie was not to be shut off in that way. He came to a stop in the hall, along which the two pairs of twins were tiptoeing their way through the house, and in the half-darkness, for the light was turned low, he pointed his fat, chubby forefinger at Flossie, holding, the while, his cigar box under his other arm.

"She did not sneeze—not a reg'lar, full, fair sneeze!" he declared. "She put her hand over her mouth an' she choked, an' she made more noise 'n if she had sneezed. Guess I know what she done!"

"*Did*, dear! *Did!*" corrected Nan. "You must use right words now that you are in regular classes at school and are out of the kindergarten. *Did*—not *done*."

"Well, Flossie *did* snort and she *did not* done sneeze," went on the fat little "fireman," as his father sometimes called him.

"I—I could 'a' sneezed if I'd wanted to," said Flossie. "Only I've an awful loud sneeze, I have. It's louder'n yours, Freddie Bobbsey."

"'Tis not!" declared Freddie. "You wait till I tickle my nose, an' I'll sneeze an' I'll show you! I'll show you who can sneeze loudest!"

"No, you will not!" said big brother Bert kindly, but firmly. "You two youngsters must keep quieter, or we can't do what we're going to do. Nan and I will take you back upstairs and mother will make you go to bed! There!"

This was such a dreadful threat, especially as Flossie and Freddie had been allowed to stay up past their regular bedtime hour on their promise to be good, that they at once quieted down.

With Bert and Nan in the lead, the smaller Bobbsey twins followed their older brother and sister. Bert reached a door opening into a large closet near the kitchen. It was in this closet that the children were to hide the things they were carrying, and why they were going to do this you will soon learn.

But just as Bert was about to open the closet door, Flossie gave a little wriggle, and, pulling her hand away from Nan—the hand that did not hold a package—the little Bobbsey girl whispered:

"It—it's goin' to be some more, Nan!"

"What is, dear?"

"My—my ker—snee—!"

The rest was a sort of gurgle, choke, and cough mingled with a sneeze. Flossie had covered her mouth and nose with one hand, and thus tried not to make as much noise as she otherwise would.

"Say! everything will be spoiled," declared Bert. "I never saw such children! We ought to 'a' made them hide their things this afternoon!"

"Flossie can't help it," said Nan kindly. "Maybe she is catching cold. I must tell mother to give her some medicine."

"'Tisn't cold," declared Flossie. "It's some dust got up my nose. There was dust in the closet where Freddie made me crawl to get him a cigar box."

"What did he want of a cigar box?" asked Nan.

"Don't tell!" cautioned Freddie. "You promised you wouldn't tell, Flossie Bobbsey!"

"All right, I won't," she promised. "Anyhow, I don't know, 'cause you didn't tell me. But I got him a box, an' it was dusty an' it makes me sneeze an'—"

"That's enough of this sneezing!" declared Bert. "Let's hide what we have and get out. Dinah's in the kitchen now, and if she hears us scuffling around she'll open the door and see us and she'll think something is going to happen."

"Well, something is going to happen," whispered Nan, with a smile. But you could not see the smile because it was rather dark in the hall. "To-morrow is Dinah's birthday, and, oh! won't she be surprised?"

"She'll be more surprised," said Freddie, though neither Bert nor Nan knew just what he meant just then. Later they did.

True enough, it was the birthday of Dinah Johnson, the fat, jolly, good-natured colored cook of the Bobbsey family, which included the four twins. Dinah's birthday was always celebrated, especially by the twins, who always brought out their presents as a sort of surprise.

This time they were bringing them down from their rooms the night before the birthday, to hide the things in a big closet near the kitchen.

Thus the gifts would be ready the first thing in the morning, to give to Dinah at the breakfast table, when daddy would call her in from the kitchen to be surprised.

It was Bert's plan thus to hide the things ahead of time, and Flossie and Freddie, of course, had begged to be allowed to take part.

"I guess she didn't hear anything," said Bert, after listening a moment, for Dinah was still in the kitchen, finishing her day's work. "The door's shut,"

Bert added. "Now then," he went on, after a pause, "let's hide our things and go back upstairs. Pass yours to me, Nan."

The older Bobbsey girl did so, and just as Bert had put away his present and hers, there was a loud sound behind him.

"What's that?" sharply whispered Bert.

"It was Freddie," answered Flossie. "An' he didn't sneeze—not at all."

"I stumbled," answered Freddie. "I'm sorry!"

"Well, it's too late for that. But I guess Dinah didn't hear," Bert said, listening a moment. "Pass me your present, Freddie, and I'll hide it with mine."

"I'll hide it myself," said the little fellow, and he made his way to the closet, squirming between Nan and Flossie.

"Oh, well, do as you please," Bert agreed. And thus it was that none of the others saw Freddie put two packages in the closet instead of one. One package was his regular present for Dinah. The other was—

But just a moment, if you please. I want to tell this story as it should be told.

Anyhow, Freddie slipped two packages into the closet without letting Bert see him. One package was a cigar box, tied with a string, and a queer scratching noise seemed to come from within it.

"There! Now everything is hid," said Bert, when Flossie's package had been put on the shelf. "Now I'll lock the door, for mother gave me the key, and Dinah can't open it. In the morning we'll give out the birthday presents."

The Bobbsey twins thought that morning would never come, but it did at last, and Dinah knew nothing of their secrets, they felt sure. With eagerness the four children assembled at the breakfast table.

"Call Dinah in, Daddy, and let us give her the things," begged Nan.

"I want to give mine first!" insisted Freddie.

"And me next," said Flossie.

Fat Dinah came waddling in, her face all smiles.

"I 'clar to goodness! Whut's gwine on now?" she asked. "Did I forgots to make de coffee, or am de toast burned?"

Dinah pretended to be very much alarmed, but I think she knew why she had been called in. At least she knew something of what was going to happen, but not all. She must have known it was her birthday, and the children always gave her something on such occasions.

"Dinah, please sit down a moment," said Mr. Bobbsey, trying not to smile. "I think Freddie has something to say to you."

"I—I got something to give you, Dinah!" cried the little fellow, hurrying out to the closet, which Bert had unlocked.

"Bress yo' heart, honey lamb! Has yo' got suffin' fo' ole Dinah?" she asked with a kind smile.

"You—you'll be s'prised," said Freddie, as he handed the fat black cook a cigar box, tied with string.

"Why, Freddie!" exclaimed Nan. "That isn't your present! Yours is wrapped in blue paper. Don't you remember? I wrapped it up for you."

"I'll give Dinah *that* present in a minute!" said Freddie, his eyes shining. "I have *two* for her!"

"Bress his heart!" murmured the cook, as she fumbled with the string.

A moment later it came off, and as the cover of the box flew open out jumped a fat little gray mouse!

"Oh, my! Oh, mah good lan'!" screamed Dinah. "Oh, a mouse! A mouse!" and she jumped up in such a hurry that she knocked over the chair on which she had been sitting.

Locked up

"Get him! Get him!" cried Bert Bobbsey, making a dive for the little mouse.

"Oh, don't let him come near me!" screamed Nan, as she left her seat and hurried over toward her mother.

"Nonsense!" exclaimed Mrs. Bobbsey. "To be frightened at a poor little mouse!"

The mouse ran under one chair after another, and circled around beneath the dining room table.

"Where's Snoop?" cried Bert, stooping down to watch which way the mouse ran. "Get Snoop in to catch the mouse!"

"Don't let him get me!" begged Flossie, and she ran over to Nan.

"Children, be quiet!" commanded Mr. Bobbsey. "All this excitement over a little mouse! Freddie, you did very wrong to put a mouse in a box and give it to Dinah for a birthday present!" and he spoke rather sternly to the little fellow.

"Am dat mouse mah birfday present?" asked the fat cook, who was huddled against the wall. "If it is I don't want it nohow!"

Isn't it queer how frightened some women and girls are of a mouse? I wonder why that it is? Anyhow, Nan, Flossie and Dinah seemed much frightened, while Bert was more interested in seeing which way the little gray creature ran.

"Get Snoop! Where is Snoop?" asked Bert, calling for the family cat. "Snoop will love to chase this mouse!"

"I help you catch my mouse for Snoop!" offered Freddie.

He had stood, eagerly waiting, to see what would happen when Dinah opened his extra present box. And enough had happened to satisfy even fun-loving Freddie.

"Here, I'll fix that mouse!" cried Mr. Bobbsey. "Let it alone, Bert. I'll drive it out!"

Mr. Bobbsey picked up a small open glass salt dish from the table, and was about to throw it at the mouse under the table.

"Don't do that," said his wife.

"Why not?" asked Mr. Bobbsey, holding the salt dish in readiness.

"Because you'll spill the salt and it will have to be cleaned up."

"I'll get the mouse!" cried Freddie. "I'll get him!"

He ran over to the goldfish tank in one corner of the room. On the table on which the tank rested was a tiny net of cloth on a handle and wire frame. Bert used the net to lift out the fish when he wanted to clean the tank, which he intended doing that day.

"I'll catch the mouse under this!" cried Freddie, grabbing up the little net and trying to dive under the table. But the little fellow slipped, and knocked over a chair. It happened to fall on Flossie's foot. Instantly the small Bobbsey girl set up a cry.

"Oh! Oh, Freddie Bobbsey! Now look what you did! My toenails is all broken! Oh! Oh!"

"Hush! Hush!" begged Mother Bobbsey, hugging Flossie.

"Oh, mah good lan'!" exclaimed Dinah, "I neber did see such a birfday as dish yeah! Nebber in all mah born days!"

Bert caught up his aluminum napkin ring and threw it across the room as the mouse made a dart toward the door leading into the kitchen.

"There he goes!" cried Bert. "No use getting Snoop now!"

"Well, I'm glad the creature is out of the way!" said Mrs. Bobbsey, with a sigh of relief. "Now, Freddie, what possessed you to do a thing like that—to give Dinah a mouse for her birthday?"

"And where did you get it?" asked Bert. "I should think you'd be afraid of it, Freddie."

"He was in the box, and I shut the cover down quick—like that"—Freddie clapped his hands together—"and I ketched him."

"You should say 'caught,'" murmured Nan. "Your teacher wouldn't like to have you say 'ketched,' Freddie."

"Well, I—I got him, anyhow," Freddie went on. "An' I tied some string around the box and I kept the mouse and I thought maybe Dinah would laugh an'—an'—"

Freddie looked around the room. All too much had happened from his little surprise. The whole place was in confusion.

"If dey is any mo' birfday presents like *dat*," said Dinah, "I reckon I better go!"

"Oh, no!" exclaimed Nan. "Mine is a nice one, Dinah!"

"So's mine!" echoed Flossie.

"An' I've another!" added Freddie. "I'm sorry I scared you, Dinah."

"Well, we'll forgive you this time," said his father. "Bring out the other presents now."

And while this is being done I will take just a moment to tell my new readers something about the children who are to be the main characters in this story.

If you have read the first book of this series, called "The Bobbsey Twins," you have learned that Mr. Bobbsey had a lumber business in the eastern city of Lakeport, on Lake Metoka. Bert and Nan were the two older twins. They had dark brown hair and brown eyes and were rather tall and slim. The younger Bobbsey twins were Flossie and Freddie. They were somewhat short and stout, and had light hair and blue eyes. The children had many good times together and with their playmates, Grace Lavine, Charlie Mason, Dannie Rugg, Nellie Parks and Ruth Nelson. They also had fun with Snoop, their pet cat, and with Snap, their dog.

There are a number of books coming between the first volume and the one just before this. The Bobbsey twins went to the country to visit Uncle Daniel, and at the seashore they stayed with Uncle William. Besides these trips the four children made a voyage on a houseboat, visited a great city, camped on Blueberry Island, went to Washington, and made a trip at sea. They had, a week or so before celebrating Dinah's birthday, returned home after some exciting times out West.

You may read about these last adventures in the book just before this present volume. It is called "The Bobbsey Twins in the Great West," and it tells how Bert, Nan, Flossie and Freddie helped solve a strange mystery about an old man.

It was now fall, and on their return from the West the Bobbsey twins had started to school again. Bert and Nan had gone into a higher grade, and Flossie and Freddie, though they were still the babies of the family, were now somewhat advanced at school, and were in regular classes, attending morning and afternoon, instead of going just in the morning, as they had done while they were still in the kindergarten.

One of the first affairs the Bobbsey twins had taken part in since their return from the West had been Dinah's birthday celebration. Each of the children had bought the cook, of whom they were very fond, a present, but Freddie had provided an extra one, as we have seen.

"Don't ever do it again, Freddie!" cautioned his father, when quiet had once more settled over the household.

"I won't, Daddy," he promised.

"Then you may give Dinah her regular present," said Mother Bobbsey.

Freddie handed the cook a package wrapped in blue paper.

"Is yo' suah dey isn't no mouse in dis?" asked Dinah, pretending to be frightened.

"No mouse!" Freddie assured her. "You open it!"

And when Dinah had done so she found a bottle of perfume, which, she declared, was "jest de sweetest kind what ebber was!" It was exactly what she had wished for, she said.

Then the other presents were given to her. Nan's was a pocketbook, and Bert's a pair of comfortable slippers. Flossie handed Dinah a gay, red silk handkerchief.

"An' when I puts pufume on *dat*, an' walks out, everybody'll be wishin' dey was me!" declared the fat, black cook. "Dish suah am a lovely birfday!"

There were presents, also, from Mr. and Mrs. Bobbsey, and when she had admired everything, and thanked them all, Dinah finished bringing in the breakfast. They all laughed at Freddie's mouse, and he told how he had caught it.

He had had some nuts in a cigar box, and the day before, coming softly up to it, he had seen a little mouse nibbling away among the nuts and shells. As quick as a wink Freddie clapped the cover down, and had caught the mouse fast. Then, without saying anything to anyone about it, he had given it to Dinah.

"Come on, Bert, or we'll be late for school!" called Nan, as she finished her breakfast.

"I'll be right with you," her brother answered. "If Charlie Mason calls tell him to wait. He and I are going fishing this afternoon."

"Can I come?" asked Freddie. "I'll help dig worms."

"Not now," Bert answered. "Maybe to-morrow."

"You wait for me, Freddie!" called Flossie.

"Yes, I'll wait," he promised.

Soon the Bobbsey twins were on their way to school. Bert walked with Charlie Mason and Dannie Rugg, while Grace Lavine and Nellie Parks strolled along with Nan.

"Did you bring your skipping rope?" asked Grace of Nan. Grace was very fond of this fun, though once she had jumped too much and had been taken ill.

"No, I didn't bring it," Nan answered. "I brought a new bean bag, though, and we can play that at recess."

"Oh, that'll be fun!" cried Nellie.

Bert and Charlie were talking about the best place to go fishing. And the younger Bobbsey twins were talking about something else.

"If he does it again to-day, you tell me an' I'll fix him," said Freddie to Flossie.

"I will," his golden-haired sister answered. "Will you make him stop, Freddie?"

"Sure I will! You come and tell me!"

"What is it you are going to do?" asked Nan of her smaller brother and sister. But just then the warning bell rang and they all had to run so they would not be late, and Nan forgot about what she had overheard.

At recess there were jolly times in the school playground. Some of the boys got up a baseball game, and others played marbles, leapfrog or mumble-the-peg. The girls skipped rope or tossed bean bags, while some played different kinds of tag. It was cool, so that running about and jumping made one feel fine.

Suddenly from the lower end of the playground, near the shed where the janitor kept his brooms, a lawnmower, and other things, came a cry of alarm.

"That's Flossie!" exclaimed Nan, pausing in the midst of a bean bag game. "Something's the matter!"

She caught sight of Flossie and Freddie in some sort of a battle with Nick Malone, one of the "bad" boys of the school. Flossie and Freddie seemed to be having a fight with Nick.

However, the battle was soon over. Before Nan reached the scene or could call to Bert to come to her help, Nick disappeared, and Flossie and Freddie, each laughing, ran over to the other side of the yard.

"Oh, I guess they are all right," said Nan, as she stopped running and turned back.

Then the bell rang to call the children in from their play, and they took their places in long lines. A little later Bert and Nan were in their room, saying their lessons, and Flossie and Freddie were with their classmates, getting ready to recite in geography.

Miss Snell, their teacher, looked over the room. She noticed one vacant seat.

"Where is Nick?" asked Miss Snell. "He was here before recess. Did anyone see him go home?"

No one answered for a moment, and then Flossie raised her little, fat, chubby hand.

"Yes, Flossie, what is it?" asked Miss Snell, with a smile.

"Nick didn't go home," said the little girl. "He—he's out in the yard."

"Out in the yard?" exclaimed the teacher. "He should come in!"

"If you please, he can't," said Freddie suddenly. "He's locked up! I locked him up!"

Thanksgiving

Miss Snell was not quite sure that she understood Freddie Bobbsey. She looked at the little twin, smiled to make him understand that she was not cross, and said:

"What did you do to Nick, Freddie?"

"I locked him up," Freddie answered. "In the tool shed. I have the key, too," and, marching up to Miss Snell's desk he laid on it a large key.

"You locked Nick in the tool shed!" repeated the surprised teacher. "Why, Freddie Bobbsey! what a strange thing to do. Why did you do it?"

"He pulled my hair," Flossie explained. "I mean Nick did. He pulled it yesterday, too, and I told Freddie and Freddie said he would make Nick stop."

"Yes, go on, please," urged Miss Snell, as Flossie grew silent.

"Well, when he pulled it again to-day," resumed the little girl, "I hollered for Freddie and we hit Nick and he hit us and we pushed him into the shed and—and—"

"I locked the door!" finished Freddie. "You can hear him hollerin' to get out," he added. "Listen!"

The windows had been opened to freshen the air in the classroom, and as silence followed Freddie's last remark Miss Snell and the children could plainly hear, coming from the shed, the voice of someone calling:

"Let me out! Let me out!"

"That's Nick," calmly explained Freddie. "But I'm not going to let him out 'cause he pulled Flossie's hair."

"Well, of course, he shouldn't do that," said Miss Snell. "But you should not have locked him in, Freddie. I shall have to tell the principal and get him to let Nick out."

The eyes of Flossie and Freddie grew big as the teacher said this. The eyes of the other children opened wide also. To have to tell "the principal" anything meant that it was very serious.

"But I am sure you did not mean to do wrong," Miss Snell added, as she saw that Freddie and Flossie looked rather frightened. "It will be all right, I'll have the principal let Nick out. You may look over your geography lesson while I am gone. I want you to tell me, when I come back, what is a river, a lake, and an island."

"We know about a island," said Flossie in a loud whisper. "Once we camped on Blueberry Island, didn't we, Freddie?"

"Yep!" he answered. "An' I fell in!"

"Well, you may tell us about that later," and Miss Snell tried not to laugh. "But don't talk any more in school; and study your lesson while I go to Mr. Nixon's office."

While Miss Snell was out of the room I do not believe much studying was done by Flossie, Freddie or any of their classmates. They all listened as, through the open window, came the cries of Nick Malone calling:

"Let me out! Let me out!"

"I locked him in—'cause he pulled Flossie's hair!" declared Freddie, and Freddie was looked upon as quite a hero by the boys and girls in his room.

By standing up, Flossie, Freddie and the others in their class could see the tool shed. And the children stood up and looked out as Miss Snell and the principal went to release the locked-up boy. He came out crying, and seemed frightened. But he soon quieted down, and promised never again to pull Flossie's hair, while Freddie was made to promise never again to lock anyone in the tool shed.

"Tell your teacher, or tell me, when anyone plagues your sister, Freddie," the principal said.

"Yes'm—I mean yes, sir," Freddie answered.

Neither he nor Flossie had any more trouble with the "bad" boy, about whose teasing they had talked on their way to school that morning. I think, after being locked up, that Nick was afraid of Freddie. At any rate, Flossie's hair was not again pulled.

"Our smaller twins are growing up," said Mr. Bobbsey to his wife at home that night, when the story of what had happened in school had been told at the supper table.

"Yes," agreed Mrs. Bobbsey. "Our little 'fireman' and our 'fat fairy' will soon be almost as big as Bert and Nan." Fireman and fairy were the pet names for the smaller Bobbsey twins. But they were getting almost too old for pet names now.

The weeks passed, and the weather grew colder, though, as yet, no snow had appeared. Freddie and Flossie, who had gotten out their sleds soon after coming home from the West, looked at the sky anxiously each day.

"Do you think it will ever snow?" asked Flossie of her mother. "I want to go coasting."

"So do I, and skating, too," Freddie added.

"Oh, there is still plenty of time for it to snow this winter," said their mother. "Why, it isn't Thanksgiving yet."

"Oh, that's so!" exclaimed Freddie. "Thanksgiving is coming, an' we'll have cranberry sauce an' turkey!"

"An' pie an' cake!" cried Flossie.

"Thanksgiving is not meant only for feasting," said their mother. "It is a time for being thankful for all your blessings. It is a time, also, to think of the poor, and to try to help them."

"I wish we could help some poor," said Flossie. "Is it fun, Mother?"

"Well, I don't know that you would call it fun," her mother replied, with a smile, "though it gives more pleasure than many things that you do call 'fun'. Just try it and see."

Rather thoughtful, Flossie and Freddie went out together. It was the Saturday before Thanksgiving and they did not have to go to school. They each had two cents to spend, and it was while going down the street to the nearest candy store that they passed the home of Miss Alicia Pompret.

"Hello, Bobbsey twins!" called Miss Pompret to Flossie and Freddie.

"Hello!" answered the blue-eyed little boy and girl. They knew Miss Pompret quite well, since Bert and Nan had, on their trip to Washington, discovered some of the elderly lady's missing valuable china. Miss Pompret was what some people would call "rich," and she had offered a reward for the finding of her rare sugar-bowl and milk-pitcher. It was these pieces that Nan had, by chance, seen in a secondhand store window, and Miss Pompret paid the older Bobbsey twins the reward, which they turned in to charity.

"Are you going to the store for your mother?" asked Miss Pompret of Flossie and Freddie, as they paused at her door.

"We're going to the store for ourselves," Freddie answered.

"We have two cents apiece," added his sister.

"Oh, I see!" laughed the elderly, maiden lady. "Well, on your way would you mind stopping at the grocer's and telling him he hasn't yet sent the barrel of flour, the barrel of potatoes, and the ten hams I ordered. Tell him I expect them to-day."

"My! you're gettin' a lot of stuff, Miss Pompret," said Flossie.

"Well, you see, I am going to give a large dinner to a number of poor people for Thanksgiving," said Miss Pompret, "and I want some things for them to take home with them. That's why I'm ordering so much."

"For the poor!" murmured Freddie.

"Yes, dear," went on the lady. "You know Thanksgiving is not meant to see how much we can eat, but to think of our blessings and help other persons to have blessings that they may be thankful for."

"That's what mother said," remarked Flossie. "Yes'm, we'll stop at the grocery for you."

"Thank you," called Miss Pompret.

Then, as she and Freddie walked on, Flossie turned to her brother and said:

"Freddie, didn't we ought to do something for the poor?"

"Maybe we ought," he agreed. "But who is poor?"

"Anybody that has ragged clothes is poor," observed Flossie. "We could give 'em some of our clothes, 'cause I've got so many my closet is full."

"I've two pair of pants," observed Freddie. "I don't need but one, I guess. But you can't eat clothes, Flossie."

"I know it, but you have to have clothes when it's cold. And it maybe will snow for Thanksgiving. Oh, Freddie! we could give our two cents to somebody poor for Thanksgiving!" Flossie's eyes were shining with delight.

"Yes, we could do that," said Freddie, slowly. "But you can't get much clothes for two cents and not much to eat, I don't guess."

Flossie thought this over for a moment, and then her face lighted up.

"I know what we can do!" she said. "We can look for some poor ragged people, and take them to our house for Thanksgiving. Mother or father could give them some clothes and they could have some of our turkey. Daddy and mother have some dressings, too, like Miss Pompret said."

"She didn't say 'dressings,'" objected Freddie. "It's 'blessings,' like you get in Sunday-school."

"Oh," said Flossie. "Well, we could get some for the poor. Let's do it, Freddie."

"All right," agreed the little fellow.

They were just going into the candy store, having stopped at the grocer's with the message from Miss Pompret, when Flossie and Freddie caught sight of a ragged boy and girl, about their own age, standing with their faces close against the glass of the show window of the toy and candy shop.

"Freddie, look!" whispered Flossie.

"They're poor!" whispered Freddie. "Let's take them!"

Flossie nodded in agreement, and then they went up to the ragged children who were eagerly gazing in the window, which was partly filled with Christmas toys.

"Come on with us," said Freddie, tapping the other boy on the shoulder.

Quickly the boy turned, doubled up his fist, and, thrusting the ragged girl behind him, he exclaimed:

"Now you let us alone! We wasn't doin' nothin'! We was just lookin' in the winder, an' that's what it's for! You let us alone!"

Bert in Danger

Flossie and Freddie were so surprised at the strange action on the part of the ragged boy that they hardly knew what to do. Flossie looked at Freddie and Freddie looked at his sister, and then they looked at the strange boy and girl.

"You let her alone, an' you let me alone!" ordered the ragged boy. "I ain't done nothin', an' she ain't done nothin'!"

"You shouldn't say 'ain't,' 'cause it ain't—I mean it *isn't* a good word. Our teacher says so," Flossie quickly admonished the strange boy.

"Well, I don't care what I say, you oughtn't to drive us away from lookin' in this winder," objected the boy. "Nice smells comes out; and when you ain't—I mean when you *isn't* got any money to buy candy, you can smell it!"

Flossie and Freddie looked at each other in surprise. To be so poor that one had to "smell" candy instead of eating it, was to be poor indeed! Flossie opened her fat chubby hand and looked at the two moist pennies clutched there. Freddie did the same. Then the small Bobbsey twins, with one accord, held out the money to the boy and girl.

"Here," said Freddie. "Take it!"

"Mine too!" added Flossie. "You can buy candy with it!"

For a moment the ragged boy and girl did not know what to say. Then a smile came over the boy's face. His fist unclenched, and his sister smiled too.

"You mean this—for us?" he asked.

"Sure!" answered Freddie. "We don't need candy, and we'll feel good for Thanksgivin'!"

"Oh, I'm going to buy two lollypops!" cried the ragged girl.

"I want gum!" said the boy, and into the store they disappeared.

Freddie drew a long breath.

"I—I feel happy, don't you?" he asked Flossie.

"Yes," she answered. "I—I guess I do! Anyhow, we can ask mother for more pennies when we go home."

"Let's take them home for Thanksgiving," suggested Freddie.

"You mean that ragged boy and girl?" asked Flossie.

"Yes. Miss Pompret is going to feed some poor, and we can feed some at our house. Let's take 'em home," went on Freddie.

"Oh, that will be fine!" Flossie agreed. "Let's!"

When they came out of the candy store the ragged boy and his sister, who at first thought Flossie and Freddie had wanted to drive them away from the window, were smiling.

"You're coming home with us!" announced Freddie, taking the boy's hand.

"For Thanksgiving," added Flossie. "Course it isn't Thanksgiving yet, but we want to feel good when it does come, so we're going to feed you now."

"Well, I'm hungry all right," sighed the ragged boy.

"So'm I," said his sister.

And so, hardly knowing what was going to happen, the ragged boy, who said his name was Dick, and his sister, who was Mary Thompson, went with the little Bobbsey twins.

Mrs. Bobbsey was very much surprised when her little son and daughter came up the steps, leading a strange ragged boy and girl.

"We brought them home for Thanksgiving, like Miss Pompret's going to do," said Freddie.

"So's to make us be more happier," added Flossie. "And we gave them our two cents, so please can we have more? And they're hungry, Mother!"

Mrs. Bobbsey understood that it was the kind hearts of Flossie and Freddie that had brought all this about. So she welcomed the two strange children, and took them out to Dinah, who, you may be sure, fed them enough, and almost too much.

After that meal, which Dick said was the "best feed" he ever had eaten, and after Flossie and Freddie had finished watching their strange, ragged guests eat, Mrs. Bobbsey asked Dick and his sister some questions.

She found out that they lived on the other side of town, that their father was dead, and that their mother did what she could for her children.

"Do you go to our school?" asked Freddie, during a pause in his mother's questions. "We've a nice school, and our teacher's name is Miss Snell, and—"

"And Freddie locked a boy up in the tool shed 'cause he pulled my hair—I mean the bad boy pulled my hair," broke in Flossie.

"We don't go to school—our clothes is too ragged," said Mary, in a low voice.

"Never mind, my dear. Perhaps I can find some clothes for you that aren't quite so full of holes," offered Mrs. Bobbsey kindly. "Clothes with holes in are fine for summer," she said, with a laugh, "but not so good for winter. I'll see what I can find."

She found some good, half-worn garments belonging to the twins, and Dick and Mary took the clothes home. The result was that they appeared at school the following Monday. But neither Flossie nor Freddie spoke of their mother having given the two fatherless children clothes to wear.

"Now we'll be happy for Thanksgiving; won't we, Freddie?" asked Flossie, when it was settled that Dick and Mary were to be taken care of.

"Yes," Freddie agreed. "And I hope we have a big turkey!"

"An' cranberry sauce!" added his sister.

There was a fine Thanksgiving dinner at the Bobbsey home, but the mother of the four twins did not forget the poor. She helped Miss Pompret with that lady's Thanksgiving feast for those who were not fortunate enough to have one of their own, and Mr. Bobbsey and some other good-hearted men of Lakeport provided money so that the Salvation Army could feed a number of hungry men who were out of work.

Still there was one reason why at least Flossie and Freddie, of the Bobbsey family, were not quite happy that Thanksgiving day. And the reason was because there was no snow. The children had polished their sleds, had wiped the rust off the runners, and were all ready for a coast. But without snow there can be no sleigh riding, and though the weather was cold, the sun shone from a cloudless sky, and Flossie and Freddie were much disappointed.

"Do you think it will ever snow, Mother?" asked Flossie for about the twentieth time.

"And will there be ice so I can skate?" Freddie wanted to know.

"Well, my dears, there will be snow and ice, surely, in a little while," answered Mrs. Bobbsey. "But when I can not say. You must be patient. Think of your blessings, as Uncle William would say."

"I want to have some fun," complained Freddie. "Oh, look!" he suddenly cried, coming back to the window away from which he had started to go.

"What is it?" asked Flossie.

"It's our cat—Snoop! A big dog just came along and Snoop ran up the tree. Now he can't get down!"

"Oh, of course Snoop can get down out of a tree," said Nan. "He's often climbed up and down before."

But this time Snoop did not come down. Whether he had been too much frightened by the dog, or whether he was afraid of falling if he started to come down backward out of the tree, I don't know. But Snoop stayed up on a limb, where he cried pitifully.

"I'll get him down," offered Bert. "I can climb out on that limb from our front porch roof. I've done it before."

Bert went upstairs, climbed out on the porch roof, and a little later was over in the tree where Snoop was perched.

"Mew! Mew!" dismally cried the cat.

"I'm coming to get you," said Bert, kindly. "Wait a minute, Snoop!"

From the ground Flossie, Freddie and Nan watched Bert make his way out on a limb toward Snoop. And then, all of a sudden, there was a cracking, breaking sound and Bert cried:

"Oh, I'm falling! I'm going to fall!"

Christmas Trees

Several things happened all in a moment. The cracking limb, Bert's cries, and the swaying of the bough as it bent toward the ground with the weight of the Bobbsey boy frightened Snoop, the cat. All this did just what was needed, for it so frightened Snoop that down he scrambled out of the tree, not caring whether or not he fell.

Bert, as soon as he felt the tree branch giving way with him, reached out his arms and grasped whatever came first to his hands. This happened to be another branch over his head, so that there he was, his feet on one limb that was slowly bending beneath his weight, and his hands grasping a branch above him.

And, to add to the excitement, Flossie and Freddie, who saw what danger Bert was in, set up a dismal crying.

"Oh, Bert's going to fall! Bert's going to fall!" yelled Freddie.

"Daddy! Mother! Dinah! Somebody! Come quick!" exclaimed Flossie. "Catch Bert before he falls!"

Nan ran out under the tree and stood with her dress held up, as she used to do when her father picked apples and dropped them down to her. Nan may have thought Bert could drop down and she would catch him, as a man jumps into a circus net from the top of the tent. But, again, perhaps Nan was so excited that she really did not know what she was doing.

However, daddy and mother came hurrying to the window, attracted by the cries of the children, and Mr. Bobbsey, seeing just what was needed, said to his wife:

"Run and tell Sam to come here with the ladder. It stands back of the chicken house."

"I will," said Mrs. Bobbsey. So, instead of running out after Mr. Bobbsey to see poor Bert dangling in the tree, she hurried to the rear door and called to Sam, who was working over Mr. Bobbsey's automobile.

"Sam! Sam! Bring the ladder out in front, quick!" cried Mrs. Bobbsey.

"Ladder! De ladder?" repeated the colored husband of fat Dinah. "Am dey a fire some place?"

"No fire!" answered Mrs. Bobbsey. "But Bert is up a tree and he is falling! Mr. Bobbsey wants the ladder to get him down! Hurry!"

"Oh!" answered Sam. Then he hurried to the chicken house, got the ladder, and hurried around to the front of the house with it.

"Can you hold on a little longer, Bert?" asked his father anxiously, as Sam began to raise the ladder up into the tree.

"I—I guess so," was the answer. "Is Snoop all right?"

"Yes, Snoop's all right. He jumped. But don't you jump!" called Nan.

"I—I won't," Bert answered.

Then his father and Sam raised the ladder up into the tree, and a few minutes later they had rescued Bert, helping him so that he could put his feet on the ladder and climb down.

"What made you go up?" asked his mother, when the excitement was all over.

"I went up after Snoop," said Bert. "A strange dog chased him up the tree."

"Well, of course, you meant to be kind," said his father. "But you must be careful when in a tree. Very often a branch may look sound and strong, as though it would hold you up. But when you step on it or pull on it, it breaks. It is always a good plan, if you climb a tree in the woods—or anywhere else—to pull on a limb to test it before you bear your full weight on it. If you hear a cracking sound it means that the branch will break."

"I heard a cracking sound," Bert said. "But that was after I got out on the limb with my feet."

"Then it was almost too late," his father said. "But remember always to test a branch before you trust yourself to it."

The Bobbsey twins and the others went back into the house, and the rest of the Thanksgiving day passed pleasantly. Snoop and Snap had been given especially good dinners in honor of the occasion.

In the morning, when Flossie and Freddie awakened, which generally happened at the same time, the little fellow ran to the window and looked out.

"Oh, look, Flossie! Look!" he cried. "Come and see!"

"Is Snoop up the tree again?" asked the little girl.

"No, but it's snowing! Snowing hard! Now we can have some fun with our sleds! Come on, we'll go coasting!"

Later the two smaller Bobbsey twins, having had their breakfasts, ran out to play in the snow. Quite a little had fallen during the night, and more was coming down. It was just about right for starting to make a coasting hill.

Not far from the Bobbsey home, on a side street, was a hill where the smaller children had their fun. Bert and Nan, with some of the older boys and girls, generally went to a longer and steeper hill some distance away. But this time Bert and Nan had not gotten out their sleds.

"I'm going to wait for Charlie Mason," said Bert. "He said he'd come over as soon as it snowed. We're going to make a bob."

"May I have a ride on it?" asked Nan. "I'll help you get some pieces of carpet to tack on if you'll let me ride."

"Sure we'll let you," agreed Bert. And then he went to telephone over to ask if Charlie were coming.

Meanwhile Flossie and Freddie and some of their friends were having fun on the small hill. Each of the smaller Bobbsey twins had a sled, and the children had races to see who would get first to the bottom of the slope. With merry shouts and laughter they played amid the swirling flakes of white snow.

The fun was at its liveliest, and Flossie and Freddie were among the merriest, when along came Nick Malone, the boy whom Freddie had locked in the tool shed at school.

"Oh, Freddie! Look!" whispered Flossie, dropping the rope of her sled and moving closer to her brother.

"What is it?" asked Freddie, for he was watching Sammie Henderson go down hill backward on a "dare."

"It's that—that bad boy!" whispered Flossie. "He might pull my hair!"

"If he does, I'll—I'll—" began Freddie, and then up swaggered Nick.

"Hu! you can't do nothin' to me now," he sneered. "There ain't no teacher or principal here! There!" and he reached over as if to pull Flossie's hair.

"You let my sister alone!" cried Freddie.

"Yah! Yah! Why don't you wear girls' dresses!" taunted Nick. "You're a girl-boy! Girl-boy!"

"I am not!" declared Freddie, while the other coasters gathered around. "You go on away!"

"I'm going to have a coast! Here, I guess I'll take this sled!" cried Nick, and before Freddie could stop him the bad boy caught Flossie's sled from the ground and ran with it toward the top of the hill.

"Here! You come back! You let my sister's sled alone!" shouted Freddie, racing after Nick.

Now Freddie was a good runner, but Nick had the start of him, and reached the top of the hill first. However, Freddie was not far behind, and no sooner did Nick throw himself flat on the little Bobbsey girl's sled, face down, than Freddie made a jump, and right on top of Nick's back he landed!

"Hi! Get off!" cried Nick, his breath rather knocked out of him, for Freddie was a fat, chubby little fellow.

"You get off my sister's sled!" demanded Flossie's brother.

But it was too late for this. It was impossible for Nick to stop now, and down the hill he coasted on Flossie's sled, with Freddie on his back, both boys coasting together!

It was a trick the children often did on the hill, and there was nothing hard about it. Only this time it happened to be an accident, and the two boys were enemies and not friends.

Freddie was so surprised at the sudden and unexpected coast that he just had to hold fast to Nick and he could say nothing more. But when the bottom of the hill was reached, Freddie, being on top, began to pound Nick's back with his two sturdy fists.

"Hey! Quit! Let me up!" begged the bad boy.

"Not till you give me my sister's sled!" insisted Freddie.

"Well, how can I give it to her when you're sittin' on me?" yelled Nick.

With that Freddie got off the other lad's back, allowing him to get up. The other boys gathered around, thinking there might be a fight. But Nick had had enough. He found Freddie braver than he had thought, and turned away, muttering:

"Aw, I only wanted a ride an' I got it!"

"Yes, and Freddie had one too!" laughed Sam Miller.

Nick walked away, and then the younger Bobbsey twins again started coasting, Freddie taking Flossie's sled back to her.

It was still snowing when noon came, and Flossie and Freddie had to go home to lunch. They found Bert and Charlie busy making a bobsled in the back yard. The older boys were fastening together their sleds by a long plank, and Nan was helping by tacking some strips of carpet on the plank.

"Oh, can we ride on that?" asked Freddie.

"Maybe," said his brother. "How's the little hill?"

"Nice," Freddie answered.

"An' you ought to've seen Nick Malone take my sled and Freddie jump on his back!" cried Flossie.

"Is that fellow bothering you two again?" demanded Bert, looking up with a hammer in his hand. "I'll get after him, that's what I will!"

"Freddie got after him," explained Flossie. "Oh, I'm so glad it snows! We're going coasting some more after dinner."

"Sure!" added Freddie.

At the dinner table Bert and Nan noticed that their father seemed worried over something. He went to the window several times to look out at the storm.

"If this keeps up the shipment will never arrive," he said to his wife.

"You mean the Christmas trees?" she asked.

"Yes," answered Mr. Bobbsey. "They are late now, and something seems to be wrong up there in the woods."

"Shan't we have any Christmas tree?" asked Freddie, who did not know just what was being talked about.

"Oh, I guess so," his father said, and again he went to look at the snow.

"Are you going to sell Christmas trees?" Bert asked. He had caught the word "shipment," and knew it had to do with some part of his father's lumber business.

"Yes, I am going into the Christmas tree business this year," said Mr. Bobbsey. "That is, I have bought a large shipment of them to be sent here to me from the North Woods. If they get here in time I can sell them and make some money. But if this snow keeps up, the carloads of trees, or the shipment, will be delayed, and if they don't get here at least a week before Christmas they will be of little use to me. But perhaps the snow will not be as heavy as I fear."

"I didn't know you sold Christmas trees," remarked Nan.

"I never did before," her father said. "It's a new business for me, and I may make a failure of it."

Then the older Bobbsey twins began to understand how it is that snow can bring pleasure to boys and girls, but may often mean trouble for older people in business.

"Well, we'll hope for the best," said Mr. Bobbsey, as he started back to the office after dinner, when the white flakes were still falling steadily. "I may have to go up to the North Woods to see about that shipment of trees if they don't get here soon."

"Could we go?" asked Bert, having a joyful vision of a mid-winter trip to one of his father's lumber camps.

"Well, I'll see," answered Mr. Bobbsey, and Nan and Bert looked at each other in delight.

Some strange adventures were ahead of them, though they did not know it.

Off to Cedar Camp

Bert and Charlie, with Nan's help, finished the bobsled in time to use on the coasting hill that afternoon and early in the evening. And it is a good thing they had hurried with it, for the next day there came a thaw and the snow began to melt. It melted so fast that by noon there was scarcely enough for Flossie and Freddie to have any fun on even the small hill, and what snow there was had mostly turned to slush.

"Oh, dear," sighed Nan, when she found that she and her brothers and sister had to give up their pleasure, "this isn't any fun!"

"That's right," agreed Bert. "But the winter isn't over. We always have a lot of snow after Christmas."

"And I suppose we ought to be glad there isn't a big storm," went on Nan, when it had been decided to give up coasting and the older Bobbsey twins were dragging home the new bobsled.

"Why ought we be glad?" Bert wanted to know.

"Because if it doesn't storm so much daddy can get his shipment of Christmas trees here and make some money."

"Oh, that's so—I forgot!" exclaimed Bert. "But if the trees do come we can't make that trip with him to the North Woods to see what the matter is. And I wanted to go on a trip like that, for we don't have much school now, on account of the holidays."

"It would be nice to go off somewhere in the winter," agreed Nan. "Remember what fun we had at Snow Lodge?"

"I should say so!" cried Bert. "But there isn't much use talking about snow when it thaws like this," and he stepped into a puddle of slush.

"Oh, be careful!" cried Nan. "You'll get your feet wet!"

"I have rubbers on," said Bert.

There was nothing to do but to leave the bobsled and the other sleds in the shed attached to the garage. There they would stay until more snow came. When Bert went into the house, after putting away the bobsled and helping Flossie and Freddie store away their smaller sleds, he found his mother waiting for him.

"Bert," said Mrs. Bobbsey, "here is a special delivery letter that just came for your father. It should have been delivered at the office, but they sent it here by mistake, and Dinah took it in before I could call to the boy to take it back with him. I called your father up about it on the telephone and he said, if you came in, to have you bring it down."

"I'll go," replied Bert cheerfully.

"Oh, may we go along?" begged Flossie.

"We'll be good!" promised Freddie.

"Shall I take them?" asked Bert of his mother.

"If you want to," she answered. "Does Nan want to go?"

But Nan, as it happened, had some sewing she wanted to do on a Christmas gift for one of her girl friends, so she said she would stay in the house and busy herself with needle and thread. Thus it came about that Bert took the smaller Bobbsey twins down to his father's office.

They went in a trolley car, and, as they always did, Freddie and Flossie became very much interested in everything that happened, from the fat lady who could hardly get on to the scenes in the streets.

There were many trucks and wagons in one street, as the car came nearer that part of Lakeport in which Mr. Bobbsey's lumberyard and office were situated. Finally the street became so crowded with wagons and automobiles that the car had to proceed slowly.

"Oh, Freddie, look!" suddenly called Flossie, pointing out of the window. A big auto-truck, piled high with crates, in which were chickens and ducks, had come to a stop alongside of the trolley car, and so close that, had the window been open, the Bobbsey twins could have reached out their hands and touched some of the fowls.

"I guess they're getting in big shipments of ducks, turkeys and chickens ready for Christmas," said Bert. "Look out there, Freddie!" he suddenly called, and, leaping from his place beside Flossie, Bert made a grab and pulled Freddie off the seat.

Only just in time, too, for at that moment the auto-truck, which had started off after being stalled, lurched to one side, and a corner of one of the chicken crates crashed through a car window, breaking the glass.

Bert had seen the crate of chickens shifting around as the truck started, and had guessed that it was going to slide over and crash against the trolley car, just as it did. So he pulled Freddie away in time.

Some of the passengers in the car screamed, and there was a shout by the conductor and motorman as the glass crashed in the electric vehicle.

And then a funny thing happened. One of the slats of the chicken crate on the auto-truck came loose, and in through the broken window fluttered a hen and a rooster. Right into the trolley they flew, the hen cackling and the rooster crowing!

"Oh, look! Look!" cried Flossie.

"Catch 'em!" shouted Freddie, pulling away from Bert and grabbing for the rooster.

But the rooster did not intend to be caught. Half running and half flying, he "scooted," as Freddie called it, down to the end of the car, and, as the conductor had just opened the door to look out and see what was causing the blockade, the rooster made his escape.

The hen, however, did not seem to know how to get out. She fluttered around, cackling and making a great fuss. The men in the car laughed, and the women held their hands over their hats so the chicken would not light on them.

"Maybe she came in here to lay an egg!" suggested Flossie, laughing.

"I'm goin' to catch her!" shouted Freddie.

"Get her and have a chicken dinner," said the motorman.

By this time the car was in an uproar, most of the passengers enjoying the queer excitement. As for the hen, I do not think she liked it at all, though she had more room than in the crate.

The driver of the auto-truck was talking to a policeman about whose fault it was that the trolley window had become broken, and the motorman and conductor now joined in.

"I've got to get that chicken and rooster back," said the truck driver. "I'll be blamed for letting them get away."

"And we'll be blamed for having a window in our car broken," said the conductor. "It was your fault."

"It was not!" insisted the driver.

Cackling and fluttering, the hen raced about inside the trolley car, and Freddie tried to catch her, but could not. Several of the men made grabs for the lively fowl, but finally she saw the same open door by which the rooster had gotten out, and away she flew.

"She didn't like it in here," observed Flossie.

"I don't blame her," said a woman passenger, laughing. "Poor thing! Her nerves must be all on an edge."

"Let's go and see if they catch 'em," suggested Freddie. But Bert said they had no time for that.

The slipping crate, which had broken the window, was finally pulled back on the truck. The slat was nailed fast so no other fowls could get out, and then the trolley car moved along. The conductor picked up the larger pieces of broken glass and pulled the curtain down over the window to keep out the cold air.

"My, you must have had some excitement," said Mr. Bobbsey, when the children finally reached his office and told him of the accident. "I'm glad Freddie wasn't cut by the broken glass."

"I'm glad, too," said the little Bobbsey boy.

Mr. Bobbsey read the letter Bert had brought him, and then the same worried look Bert had seen before came over his father's face.

"Do you want me to tell mother anything?" asked Bert.

"No, except to thank her for sending me down this letter. Still, you might say to her that I think I shall have to go to Cedar Camp in a day or two."

"Where's Cedar Camp?" asked Bert.

"Where the Christmas trees grow," his father answered, with a smile. "It's where the Christmas trees grow that I hope to have to sell. I haven't got them yet, and I'm going there to see what the trouble is. This letter is about the trees."

"Oh, can't we go and see where the Christmas trees grow?" begged Flossie.

"We like it in the woods," said Freddie.

"I suppose you do," his father answered, smiling. "But the woods in winter are very different from in summer. However, we shall not have any bad storms or severe weather for another month, I think. Perhaps I might be able to take my Bobbsey twins to Cedar Camp," and he playfully pinched Flossie's fat cheek.

"It would be nifty to go!" said Bert. "Do you really think you'll take us?"

"We'll talk it over to-night at home," said his father. "Here, take Flossie and Freddie to the store and get them some hot chocolate," he added, giving Bert some money.

The little Bobbsey twins liked the chocolate very much, but they were so excited, thinking about a possible trip to the North Woods, that they talked of nothing else.

"Do you really think you will have to go?" asked Mrs. Bobbsey of her husband that evening.

"Yes," he answered. "Those Christmas trees have been lost somewhere between Cedar Camp and here, and I must find them, or I shall lose a lot on them. I will go to Cedar Camp in a few days."

"And take us?" asked Bert.

"All of us!" cried Freddie.

Mr. and Mrs. Bobbsey looked at one another.

"Would you like to go?" asked Mr. Bobbsey of his wife.

"Where could we stay?" she inquired.

"There is a large log cabin that one of my foremen used to live in," Mr. Bobbsey answered. "The cabin is empty, and we could stay there as long as the weather did not get too cold, and as long as there were no bad storms. I really ought to go right to the woods, so that if I cannot get on the track of the lost shipment of Christmas trees I can start the men to cutting others. So we might as well all go."

"Oh, what fun!" cried the Bobbsey twins.

Since that first fall of snow, which did not last very long, there had been no storms in the region of Lakeport, and Mr. Bobbsey thought he could get to Cedar Camp and return with his family before the really severe winter weather set in. He did not believe it would take long to look up the matter of the delayed shipment of the Christmas trees and straighten it out.

So it was settled, and a few days later, when plans had been completed, the Bobbsey family started for Cedar Camp.

In the North Woods

"It's just lovely to take a trip like this," said Nan, as she leaned back in the automobile.

"Swell, I call it," declared Bert.

Flossie and Freddie said nothing just then. They were too busy looking from the windows.

Mr. Bobbsey owned a large, closed automobile, which even had an arrangement for heating, and it was just the proper vehicle for a trip like this. It easily held all the Bobbseys and their baggage, which had been piled in to go with them.

It had not taken long to make preparations for the trip. Dinah and Sam would be left in charge of the Lakeport house, and would care for Snoop and Snap.

"I wish we could take our cat along," sighed Flossie.

"And Snap would be just right for the woods," said Freddie. "Everybody has a dog in the woods."

"We haven't time to bother with Snoop and Snap now," said Mrs. Bobbsey, so the dog and cat had been left at home, as much to their sorrow as to that of the Bobbsey twins.

Cedar Camp was in what was called the "North Woods," about forty or fifty miles from Lakeport. It was a wild, desolate region, especially in the winter. In summer many camping parties made the place more lively.

Mr. Bobbsey owned some timberland there, from which was cut some of the lumber he used in his business. And it was only this year that he had decided to go into the Christmas tree trade. He had ordered many hundreds of the small cedars, spruce, and hemlocks cut and shipped to him, some to Lakeport and others to a more distant and larger city.

But something had gone wrong with the carloads of trees. They had started from Cedar Camp all right, but that was the last heard of them.

"I can trace them from the North Woods end better than from down here," Mr. Bobbsey had said, as a reason for making the trip.

The men who went into the woods to cut timber and Christmas trees had to stay in winter camps. They lived in log or slab cabins, and there were many of them scattered through the North Woods. It was in one of these cabins, which had formerly been used by a foreman and his family, that Mr. Bobbsey planned to have his wife and children stay for about a week. It would take him that long, he thought, to locate the missing Christmas trees.

And so now the Bobbsey twins were on the first part of their journey in the large, closed automobile. It was almost as comfortable as traveling in a Pullman railroad car, and it was much more fun, the children thought.

They had brought with them plenty of lunch, some extra wraps, and some blankets and bed-clothes.

"What shall we eat when we get to the North Woods?" asked Freddie, as he munched some cookies his mother passed to him and Flossie. "Shall we have any—chicken?"

"If we could 'a' brought the one in the trolley car we could," suggested Flossie. "Wasn't she funny, an' the rooster, too?"

"I wish we could 'a' caught them," Freddie murmured.

"Oh, I think we'll have enough to eat without those fowls," said their mother.

"They will if they like baked beans," said Mr. Bobbsey. "The lumbermen have plenty of those. They bake big pans of them."

"I'll help mother cook," offered Nan.

"There will be a woman at the camp to cook," Mr. Bobbsey explained. "I wrote up and engaged the wife of one of the lumbermen," he said. "I thought you'd like a little rest from looking after housework even in camp," he said to his wife.

"Thank you, I will," she said. "It will be quite nice to be in the woods in winter; especially the Christmas tree woods, where there is so much greenery."

On went the automobile, driven by Mr. Bobbsey. Lakeport was left behind and they were on a country road. The weather was fine, with hardly a cloud in the sky, and Mr. Bobbsey was glad that he had taken his family on this little trip.

It looked as though they were going to have good luck all the way. Noon came and saw them more than half over their journey, and as yet no mishaps had befallen them. There was no tire trouble and the engine of the big automobile seemed glad to work as hard as it could going up hill and on the level with the Bobbsey twins.

Mr. Bobbsey planned to get to Cedar Camp before dark, and he would have done so but for a little accident. They had left the town of Bunkport, which was the last village before the North Woods was reached, when the motor began to chug in a queer manner.

"What's that?" asked Mrs. Bobbsey. "One of the cylinders seems to be missing."

The Bobbsey twins knew what this meant. That one of the parts of the automobile engine was not working properly.

"Oh, Daddy!" exclaimed Freddie.

"I guess the spark plug needs cleaning," said Mr. Bobbsey. "But we won't stop for that now. I think we can reach Cedar Camp, and then I'll have plenty of time to take it out and look at it."

But the automobile continued to go more and more slowly, and once, on a hill, it almost stopped.

"If we can get over the top we can coast down and soon be in Cedar Camp," said Mr. Bobbsey, in answer to an anxious look from his wife.

The car did manage to climb the hill, and then it was easy to go down the other side. But there was still a farther distance to go than Mr. Bobbsey had thought. The night settled down, it became dark, and then, suddenly, when the car was on a rough road in a sort of lane cut through the evergreen trees, the engine, with a sort of cough and chug, stopped altogether.

"Oh, dear!" exclaimed Mrs. Bobbsey. "We're stalled!"

"Looks like it," said Mr. Bobbsey, preparing to get out and see what the trouble was.

"Where are we?" asked Bert, getting ready to follow his father and help if he could.

"We're in the North Woods," answered Mr. Bobbsey. "Several miles from Cedar Camp, I'm afraid."

"It—it's awful dark!" whispered Flossie. "Aren't they going to turn on the lights?"

"There aren't ever any lights in the woods 'ceptin' fireflies, are there, Daddy?" asked Freddie.

"Only our auto lights," answered his father. "Well, we may be able to travel soon."

As he was getting out of the car into the dark road, a mournful, shrill cry that echoed all about sounded through the forest.

"What's that?" gasped Nan, shrinking close to her mother. "Oh, what is it?"

A Nutting Party

Mrs. Bobbsey was rather alarmed at what had happened to the automobile to cause it to stop. She was also worried, thinking perhaps they all might have to stay out in the woods all night, if they could not go on to camp. So when Nan asked the cause of the strange noise her mother did not at first answer.

The sound came again, just as Bert was getting down out of the car to go to his father, who had lifted the hood over the motor to see what was wrong, and the strange sound so startled this Bobbsey twin lad that he let go his hold of the side of the car and slid with a bump to the ground.

"Ugh!" grunted Bert, as he fell.

He grunted in such a funny way, and he looked so odd sitting there in the dusk, as if he did not know what had happened, that Flossie and Freddie laughed. And this laughter seemed to make them less afraid of the queer call of the woods.

"Hurt yourself, Bert?" asked his father, looking up from his task of throwing the gleams of a flashlight in among the parts of the automobile motor.

"No, sir," Bert answered. "I just sat down sudden, that's all. But what was that noise, Daddy? Is it—"

As if finding fault because the Bobbsey twins had come to Cedar Camp, once more the warning call came.

"There it goes again!" exclaimed Nan.

Flossie and Freddie shrank closer to their mother, and even Nan seemed a little afraid, but Mr. Bobbsey only laughed.

"That's a hoot owl—or a screech owl, I don't know which," he said. "Anyhow, it's only a bird with feathers and big, staring eyes. And, very likely, it's looking down at us now and wondering what we're doing in his woods."

"Is the owl looking at us now?" asked Freddie, climbing away from his mother and venturing to the door of the car.

"Very likely," his father said. "But the chances are you can't see it. Owls keep pretty well hidden when there's any daylight left."

"Well, the light is fast fading," said Mrs. Bobbsey. "It's getting dark very fast, Dick. And unless we get to camp soon—well, you know what may happen," she said to her husband. "Do you think you can get the motor to going?"

"I think so," he answered. "Bert, please come here and hold the light for me."

Glad to be of help to his father, Bert arose from the ground, to which he had slipped when the sudden noise of the owl startled him, and went to hold the flash lamp. As he sent the beam moving about, in order to direct it just where his father wished it, there was a whirr and a flutter in the almost leafless branches of the trees overhead, and Flossie cried:

"There it is!"

"Yes, that's Mr. Owl," laughed her father. "He came up to look at us, but he doesn't like our bright light, because it hurts his eyes. So he flew away. Now come on, Bert, and we'll get the motor to running again. They'll be anxious at Cedar Camp if we don't get there soon."

"Do they expect us?" asked Nan.

"Oh, surely," said her father. "Hold the light steady, Bert."

The Bobbsey twin lad did as requested, and after a little examination, his father exclaimed:

"I see what the trouble is—a loose wire on a spark plug! That's easily fixed. We'll be traveling on again in a few minutes."

And so they were. Once the wire was fastened in place, the automobile could go again. Bert and his father got back in, there was a chugging and throb of the motor, and off they went through the woods, the two headlights gleaming along the dark road in the midst of the trees.

"I wish we could have arrived by daylight," said Mr. Bobbsey, as he carefully steered the car. "Cedar Camp looks ever so much better then."

"I'm glad to get here at all—so we don't have to stay out in the woods all night," said Mrs. Bobbsey.

"It would be fun to be out in the woods all night—if owls didn't bite you—wouldn't it, Flossie?" asked Freddie.

"Yes, I guess maybe," answered the little girl. "But I'd rather be in our camp an' have something to eat."

"I guess I would, too," agreed Freddie.

"Well, here we are, then. Cedar Camp!" suddenly cried Mr. Bobbsey, and, almost before the twins knew it, the car had turned from the dense woods and was in a clearing, or place where many trees were chopped down.

Around the clearing were many log cabins, and inside some of them, and outside others, lanterns were glowing, so the place was quite light, compared to the darkness of the forest.

"Cedar Camp!" cried Bert. "Is this it?"

"Yes," his father answered. "Here we are—a little late, but better late than never! Now to find our cabin."

He guided the car into the midst of the clearing, and the children could see the various cabin doors opening and men and women looking out.

"That you, Mr. Bobbsey?" a voice called.

"Yes, Jim Denton," was the answer. "We're here!"

"Thought maybe you'd given up and wouldn't get here until to-morrow," the voice went on.

As the car stopped the Bobbsey twins saw a tall, lanky man, wearing rough clothes, but whose face had a kind smile and whose blue eyes looked laughingly at them. He stood at the side of the car, peering in.

"We did have a little trouble," said Mr. Bobbsey. "And one of your owls seemed to think we hadn't any right in the woods. But here we are!"

"One of the owls, eh?" laughed Jim Denton, the foreman of the Christmas tree and lumber camp. "Well, they sure are queer birds! Make an outlandish racket, sometimes. But come on in. Your place is all ready for you, and Mrs. Baxter has had supper ready for some time."

"That's good!" exclaimed Mrs. Bobbsey. "The children are half starved, I fancy."

"Run your car over to the shed," said the foreman to Mr. Bobbsey. "It'll be safe there if it snows."

"Had any snow up here yet?" asked the father of the twins.

"Not yet, but it may come any day. I heard you had a little down your way."

"But it didn't last very long," Freddie chimed in. "We didn't have much coasting at all!"

"You didn't, eh?" laughed Jim, as he lifted out Flossie and Freddie, Bert and Nan being too big for this attention. "Well, when we do get snow up here we generally get a lot, and it may come any time. But the longer it holds off the better we can get out lumber and Christmas trees."

"What about my Christmas trees?" asked Mr. Bobbsey. "That's what I came up about."

"It is queer about those trees," said the foreman, as he helped Mrs. Bobbsey out. "We sent a lot off from here, but they must be stuck somewhere on the railroad down below. However, if they're lost we can cut more. There's plenty in the woods."

Mrs. Bobbsey and the children waited until Mr. Bobbsey had put the car under a shed, and then, when he joined them, the family, led by the foreman, walked toward the largest cabin in the clearing. This was to be the home of the Bobbseys while they were at Cedar Camp.

"Well, I am glad to see you folks!" exclaimed Mrs. Baxter, who was to do the cooking and help Mrs. Bobbsey during the stay in camp. "I began to be afraid that something had happened."

"A wire came loose," said Freddie. "But daddy soon fixed it. And we heard an owl hoot. Do you like owls?"

"Well, not specially," answered Mrs. Baxter, with a laugh.

"I don't, either," said Flossie.

The Bobbsey twins looked about the cabin that was to be their home for a time. It was a large one, and had been used by a former foreman with a large family. There were several bedrooms and it had many of the comforts of life, even though it stood in the North Woods.

Mrs. Baxter was the wife of one of the men employed in cutting down trees, and she had agreed to cook for the Bobbseys during their stay. She and her husband lived in one of the smaller cabins, and her grown daughter would cook for Mr. Baxter while his wife was with the Bobbseys.

"Now get your things off and sit right up to the table," cried Mrs. Baxter. "The supper's sort of spoiled, keeping so long."

"I fancy the twins are hungry enough to eat almost anything," said their mother. "I know I am!"

In spite of what Mrs. Baxter said, the supper proved to be very good indeed, and Flossie and Freddie passed their plates back so often to be filled again that their father said:

"My goodness! there won't be anything left for breakfast."

"Won't there, Mother?" asked Freddie anxiously, pausing with his fork half way to his mouth.

"Oh, yes! Of course! Your father's only joking!" she said, with a laugh. "But don't eat too much."

"I want just a little more," begged Flossie.

"Can we go out and look at the camp after supper?" Bert wanted to know.

"You can't see much by lantern light," his father told him. "You'll have plenty of chances to-morrow and the next few days."

Bert found it too dark out of doors when he took a look after leaving the table, and decided to wait until morning.

The cabin was warm and cosy, and the Bobbsey twins thought they had never come to a more delightful place than Cedar Camp. They sat and talked a little while after the meal, and then, when Flossie and Freddie began to show signs of being sleepy, their mother said it was time for them to go to bed. Bert and Nan soon followed.

It seemed to be the middle of the night when Flossie, awakened from a sound sleep, heard a great noise and loud shouting outside the log cabin.

"Mother! Mother! What's that?" she whispered.

"Only the lumbermen going to work," Mrs. Bobbsey answered.

"Do they go to work in the night?" Flossie wanted to know.

"It's almost morning—the sun will soon be up," her mother told the little girl. "Keep quiet and don't awaken Freddie."

Flossie turned over and closed her eyes, thinking it strange that men should have to get up and go to work in the night. It was dark, and the stars were shining, as she could see by a glimpse through her window.

"I guess maybe they're like Santa Claus," thought Flossie. "They have to go out to cut Christmas trees in the dark, same as St. Nicholas comes to our house in the dark on Christmas Eve."

Content with this thought, the little girl fell asleep, not to awaken again until it was broad daylight. She found that all were up save Freddie and herself, but the youngest Bobbsey twins soon joined the others at the breakfast table.

"Oh, goodie!" cried Freddie, when he understood that Mrs. Baxter was baking buckwheat cakes and had maple syrup to pour over them. "That's what I like!"

"He can't like 'em all, can he, Mother?" cried Flossie. "I can have some pancakes, can't I?"

"Hush! There'll be plenty for all of you!" said Mrs. Bobbsey. "What will Mrs. Baxter think?"

"I'll think they're good and hungry; and that is what I like to see when I'm baking cakes," laughed the good-natured cook. She was almost as nice as Dinah, Freddie whispered to Flossie.

"An' if she has a birthday we—we'll give her something," whispered Flossie.

"Yes," agreed Freddie, holding out his plate for another cake.

After breakfast Mrs. Bobbsey took the children for a walk in the woods around the camp, while Mr. Bobbsey went to talk with some of his lumbermen about the missing Christmas trees.

"Don't go too far away," he called to his wife.

"Why not?" she asked.

"Because the woods here are rather wild, and you and the children might get lost. There aren't many trails, paths, or roads. Keep close to camp."

"I will," she promised.

It was wonderful and beautiful in the North Woods, even though winter was at hand. Most of the birds had gone, and about the only trees that had any leaves on were the oaks. An oak tree holds many of its leaves all winter, the old ones being pushed off in the spring as the new ones come on. But there were so many spruce, pine, hemlock, and cedar trees growing all about—trees which remain green from one year to the other—that the woods were not as bare and dreary as are most forests. Cedar Camp was indeed a green Christmas camp, and a most lovely place.

"We'll have lots of fun here!" cried Freddie, running to the edge of a little hill.

"Lots of fun!" agreed Flossie. "We'll—" and then she stopped suddenly, for Freddie did a queer thing—or at least a queer thing happened to the little fellow. His feet seemed to slide out from under him, and down the hill he went, almost as though sliding on the ice!

"Oh, look! Look!" cried Flossie. "What made him do that?"

"I slid! I slid! Oh, I had a slide! I'm going to slide it again!" cried Freddie, jumping up and scrambling to the top of the hill again. "Come on, Flossie!"

"What makes him slide, Mother?" asked Flossie, as she saw her little brother go down the hill standing up, just as he and his small sister had often done on a snowy, icy slope.

"It's the pine needles," said Mrs. Bobbsey. "The ground is covered with the long, brown, smooth pine needles, and they make a slippery carpet. You may slide on them. If you fall you won't be hurt."

Soon the two smaller Bobbsey twins were having great fun sliding down the slippery pine-needle-covered hill, and Bert and Nan also took their turns.

But after two or three slides Bert found something on the ground that made him exclaim in delight and run to his mother to show her.

"Look!" he cried. "A chestnut! Are there chestnuts in these woods?"

"Yes, I did hear your father say something about them," Mrs. Bobbsey replied.

"Oh, let's hunt for some!" cried Nan.

"We'll help!" added Flossie and Freddie, deserting the pine-needle slide for the joys of nutting.

But though the twins looked in all directions they found only a few scattered chestnuts.

"The squirrels have picked up most of them," said Jim Denton, coming along a little later. "But there's a chestnut grove not far away, up Pine Brook, and there ought to be plenty left if you don't wait too long."

"Oh, Mother! may Nan and I go chestnutting?" asked Bert. "I want to get a lot!"

"Will it be safe for them?" asked Mrs. Bobbsey of the foreman.

"Oh, yes," answered Jim. "It isn't more than a mile and the trail is plain. I'll tell 'em how to go and show 'em the way."

And so, the next morning, Bert and Nan started off on a chestnut party, little dreaming of the strange things that were to happen to them and the other Bobbsey twins.

Sawmill Fun

Flossie and Freddie had teased to be allowed to go nutting with Bert and Nan, especially when the smaller Bobbsey twins learned that their brother and sister were to take a lunch and perhaps stay all the rest of the day in the woods.

"Oh, I want to go nutting!" cried Flossie.

"So do I!" wailed Freddie. "An' I want to eat my dinner under the Christmas trees!"

"We can't have any fun if they come with us," objected Bert, in a whisper to his mother.

"We'll take them some other time," added Nan. "They'd get tired and want to come back before we found any nuts, Mother."

"Yes," said Mrs. Bobbsey, "perhaps they would. You can take them some other time, I suppose." Then, as she knew Flossie and Freddie would be disappointed, Mrs. Bobbsey called to them:

"Come, little twins, we'll go down to the sawmill and see the big logs sawed up into boards. Maybe you can ride on the log carriers."

Flossie and Freddie knew what this was, and to them there was no better fun. Also they liked to see the big, jagged-tooth saw whizzing about and cutting its way through the logs with such a queer, ripping, buzzing sound.

"Oh, if we can go to the sawmill that will be 'most as much fun as nutting," agreed Freddie.

"Will you bring us some nuts?" asked Flossie.

"Yes," promised Nan. "And next time we go we'll take you."

So the nutting party was arranged. Taking lunch was a sort of afterthought on the part of Bert.

"What'll we do if we get hungry?" he had asked his mother.

"We'll take something to eat in our pockets," Nan had said.

"I'm going to eat mine outside—sitting on a log!" laughed Bert.

"Smarty!" laughed Nan. "I'll catch you next time!"

Mrs. Baxter put up for the children a good lunch, more than enough for two meals, Mrs. Bobbsey said.

"But we'll get awful hungry in the woods," Bert remarked. "And we don't want to have to eat the nuts we get."

True to his promise, Jim Denton, the foreman, showed the older Bobbsey twins where to take the path that led up along Pine Brook and deeper into the forest about Cedar Camp, where the chestnut trees were growing.

"Good-bye!" called Flossie and Freddie, as they stood on the porch of the log cabin, waving to Bert and Nan, who started off with their lunch to be gone the rest of the day on the nutting party.

"Good-bye," echoed the older Bobbsey twins, and then they were soon lost to sight in the turn of the path along Pine Brook, which led deeper into the North Woods.

"Now for some sawmill fun!" called Mrs. Bobbsey. "We'll go down and see the little saw chew up the big logs."

In addition to sending to market logs for telegraph poles and the masts of ships, Mr. Bobbsey's men in the North Woods also sawed up trees into planks and boards which were sold in the neighborhood. Besides this there was the Christmas tree trade, but that only took place at this time of year, around the holidays.

Flossie and Freddie were too small to think much about the missing Christmas trees, which their father had come to camp to see about. All they were anxious for was to have some fun, and going to the sawmill was part of this.

The sawmill was farther down on Pine Brook, where that stream widened out and was dammed up to make a waterfall. Part of the waterfall went through a flume, or sort of wooden canal, and the water, falling down a shaft, or wooden tunnel standing on end, turned a turbine wheel.

A turbine wheel is quite different from the ordinary mill wheel you may have seen. In fact you can not see the turbine wheel at all, for it is closed in at the bottom of the water shaft. It is small, but very powerful, and it was this kind of wheel which turned the saw machinery in Mr. Bobbsey's Cedar Camp mill.

Before the smaller Bobbsey twins reached the mill they could hear the ripping, tearing sound of the saw as it cut its way through the logs, slicing them into boards as your mother slices the loaf of bread with the carving knife.

"Good morning, Mrs. Bobbsey—also little twins!" called Foreman Tom Case, who had charge of the sawmill. "Did you come to buy some lumber this morning?"

Flossie and Freddie knew Tom Case, for he had, at one time, worked in the lumberyard of their father in Lakeport, so it was meeting an old friend to see him here.

"Do you want one or two million feet this morning, Flossie?" asked the jolly sawman. "And will you take it with you or have it sent?"

"I guess we'll just take some sawdust for Flossie's doll," laughed Freddie. This was a standing joke between the sawmill man and the little twins. Tom Case was always trying to sell a big lot of lumber to Flossie and Freddie, and they always said all they wanted was a little sawdust.

"Oh, shucks! you aren't any kind of customers to have around a lumber camp," laughed Mr. Case. "Where's the rest of the family?" he asked Mrs. Bobbsey.

"Bert and Nan have gone nutting," their mother answered. "So we came down here to see what was going on."

"Well, we're sawing up a lot of logs to-day," said the head man of the mill. "Here, you twins sit right down on this soft place, and you can watch everything." Mr. Case spread a horse blanket on top of a pile of soft, fragrant sawdust, and on this Mrs. Bobbsey and the smaller twins sat down.

They saw the lumber men float logs down into the pond at one side of the dam and near the flume through which the water dropped to turn the turbine wheel. Into these logs a big iron hook was driven. The hook was fast to a chain, and the chain was wound around a drum, or big roller.

When a man threw over a lever that started the machinery, the drum turned, the chain was wound up and the log was pulled from the water up on land and ready to be put on the moving carriage which fed it into the teeth of the saw.

"Could we ride on the logs?" cried Flossie, as she saw them pulled, or "snaked," as it is called, out of the pond and up on shore.

"Yes! Yes!" chimed in Freddie.

"Oh, no," his mother answered. "You might roll off, and if the log turned over, and got on your legs, it would break them. It wouldn't be safe—see there!"

One of the lumbermen had jumped on top of a log that was being pulled along by the chain. For a time he kept his balance, and was given a ride. But as Mrs. Bobbsey cried out, the log struck a stone and turned over, and if the lumberman had not jumped he would have been thrown.

He leaped to one side with a laugh, and ran into the mill.

"That's what might have happened to you, only you might not have gotten off so easily," said Mrs. Bobbsey.

"I'd like to ride," sighed Flossie.

"So would I!" added Freddie.

"Let 'em ride on the log carriage. That's safe if they don't get too near the saw, and you can ride with them and watch," said Tom Case.

"All right," agreed Mrs. Bobbsey.

The log carriage was a movable platform of framework, on which the logs rested as they were sawed into boards. The logs were rolled up on the carriage by men, when the machinery had been stopped and the big buzz saw was no longer whirring around. Once a log was fastened in place, Tom Case pulled a lever, and the turbine wheel began to turn the saw, and also move forward the carriage. The carriage, or framework carrying the log, moved slowly forward by means of cogwheels underneath, so that it fed the log into the teeth of the saw which ripped off wide planks and boards.

Mrs. Bobbsey and the little twins sat on the far end of the carriage, and began to ride forward with it. Of course if they had stayed on too long they would have been carried up against the dangerous saw just as the log was. But before this would happen they could step off, as the carriage moved slowly, like an automobile just before it stops.

"Oh, this is fun!" cried Flossie, as she dragged her feet through little piles of sawdust.

"'Most as much fun as nutting!" agreed Freddie. "I'm going to be a lumber-saw man when I grow up."

"Then you aren't going to be a fireman?" asked his mother, for that had been Freddie's great ambition.

"Nope; I'm going to have a sawmill," he decided. But as he changed his mind about every other day concerning what he intended to do when he grew up, his mother did not take him seriously this time.

She and the twins rode on the log carriage until the big tree length was almost sawed through, and then she helped Flossie and Freddie off. With a final zip and clatter the board was sawed off the side of the log. Then the carriage would move back its full length, the log would be shifted over to enable the saw to cut a new place, and the work would start over again.

The log carriage moved backward, when no sawing was being done, much faster than it moved forward. And the little Bobbsey twins liked this backward ride very much, as they went fairly whizzing along.

"All aboard!" called Tom Case, as he prepared to send the carriage on its return trip. Mrs. Bobbsey and Flossie and Freddie took their places.

There was a rattle and a rumble, and back they shot, the twins shouting in glee and kicking aside the piles of sawdust. Thus they had great fun at the sawmill, and they did not want to come away when the noon whistle blew and it was time for lunch. For there was a steam engine in Cedar Camp, as well as the turbine wheel, and this steam engine had a whistle which the engineer blew to tell the men to stop for dinner.

After dinner Mrs. Bobbsey went to lie down, and after cautioning Flossie and Freddie not to go near the sawmill without her, she left the smaller twins to amuse themselves near the cabin. Their father was out with some of his men looking after Christmas trees, and as Bert and Nan had gone nutting, Flossie and Freddie looked about to find some amusement of their own.

"Let's play sawmill!" proposed Freddie, as he and Flossie wandered down near Pine Brook, where it ran over the dam, making a waterfall.

"All right," agreed the little girl. "But what'll we have for a saw?"

Freddie looked around and noticed a wheelbarrow not far off.

"That'll do," he said. "We'll turn it downside up, and I'll turn the wheel for a saw and you can hold sticks against it and make believe they're being sawed up."

"All right," agreed Flossie. "That'll make a fine saw."

They went over to the wheelbarrow, and then a new idea came to Freddie.

"Oh, Flossie!" he cried, "you sit in it and I'll wheel you down to the edge of the brook. We'll have our sawmill there, and make believe to snake logs out of the water like Mr. Case did."

This suited Flossie exactly, and soon she had taken her place in the wheelbarrow. Freddie grasped the handles, but his sister was almost more of a load than he had bargained for. Still he was a sturdy little chap, and he managed to stagger on, wheeling Flossie toward the brook.

There was a smooth place on a little knoll near the brook where Freddie intended to set up his wheelbarrow sawmill. Toward this place he wheeled Flossie, and all might have gone well had it not been for the fact that the ground was covered with those slippery pine needles.

Freddie managed to wheel his sister up the slope, and he was just going to set the barrow down and tell Flossie to get out so he could turn it over and make a saw of it, when his feet slipped. He lurched forward, gave the wheelbarrow a push, and, an instant later, it turned over, and Flossie, sliding on the slippery, brown pine needles, began to go down the slope and straight toward the brook, just back of the dam.

Freddie, too, sat down hard and suddenly, but though the breath was knocked out of him for a moment, he managed to pick himself up and to cry:

"Mother! Mother! Come quick! Flossie's fallen into the brook and she'll be carried over the dam!"

And, as he called, into the water at the foot of the pine needle hill splashed poor Flossie Bobbsey!

A Sudden Storm

While Flossie and Freddie were having such fun at the real sawmill, and before Freddie had, by accident, upset Flossie down the pine needle bank into the brook above the mill dam, Bert and Nan were trudging along through the woods on their way to the chestnut grove, about which Jim Denton had told them.

"Aren't you glad we came to Cedar Camp, Bert?" asked Nan.

"I sure am!" answered her brother. "It's like having two vacations in the same year. We had fun out West, and we'll have fun here."

"We can have a party when we get back, and roast the chestnuts," suggested Nan.

"I hope we get a lot," went on Bert, kicking aside the pine cones and dried leaves. "We'll want some for Flossie and Freddie."

"Yes, and for daddy and mother," added Nan. "They like chestnuts, too."

The day had started as a bright and sunny one, though it was colder up here in the North Woods than down in Lakeport. But Bert and Nan were warmly dressed, and they were so accustomed to being out of doors that a little cold did not bother them.

But though the sun had shone brightly when they had started on their nutting trip, they had not gone far before the sky began to be overcast with clouds. Not that Bert and Nan minded this. They were too busy looking for chestnut trees and thinking what a good time they were having to mind the weather.

For it was fun just to walk through the woods and breathe the sweet, spicy odors of the pine and cedar trees. The ground underfoot was thickly carpeted with dried leaves and pine needles, so that the footfalls of the older Bobbsey twins made scarcely any sound as they walked along.

It was so quiet that the children heard many sounds in the forest which was all about them. They were following a path that led along Pine Brook, and Jim Denton had said that if they kept to this path they would come after about a mile's walk to a grove of chestnut trees.

"And if you don't find any nuts there, keep on a little farther," the lumberman had said. "The squirrels and chipmunks can't have taken all of them."

So interested were Bert and Nan that they paid little attention to the weather. In fact, they could scarcely see the sky at times. This was because the cedar and other trees were so thick overhead.

As they were going along the path where the pine needles made a thicker carpet than usual, Bert, who was in the lead, came to a sudden stop.

"What's the matter?" asked Nan, shifting from one hand to the other the bundle of lunch she carried.

"I thought I heard something," said Bert in a low voice.

A moment later there was no doubt of this, for both he and his sister heard a grunting noise in the bushes, and then they heard the rustle of dried leaves and the snapping of twigs.

"Oh, Bert! Maybe it's a bear!" cried Nan, clinging to her brother.

"A—a bear!" gasped Bert. He hardly knew what else to say.

"Oh, look!" gasped Nan. She pointed toward a bush, and, coming out from under it, was a little animal, somewhat larger than a rabbit, but with different kind of fur, small ears, and with a tail that seemed to have rings of fur around it.

"It's a little bear!" gasped Nan. "Oh, Bert! we'd better run back to camp before the big bear comes."

Bert looked at the furry animal, whose bright eyes peered at the Bobbsey twins, and then Nan's brother laughed.

"I know what it is!" he said. "It's a raccoon. I can tell by the rings on its tail."

"A raccoon!" gasped Nan. "Will it—will it hurt us?"

"No," answered Bert, and this was borne out a moment later, for with a snorting grunt the raccoon turned and scurried away into the bushes.

"There!" said Bert. "He's gone!"

"I'm glad of it," returned Nan, with a sigh of relief. "I don't like raccoons when I'm chestnutting."

"They're nice!" declared Bert. "I wish I could see him again."

But the raccoon did not show itself, probably being just as much frightened at having seen the Bobbsey twins as Nan was at getting a glimpse of the ring-tailed creature.

Over this little fright, the Bobbsey twins walked on again, and soon they had reached the grove that the foreman had told them about.

"This must be the place—there are chestnut trees here," said Bert. His father had taught him how to tell the more common sorts of trees by means of their leaves and bark.

"Well, let's look for chestnuts," proposed Nan.

With sticks the children began poking among the leaves, turning them over, for the little brown nuts, when the frost has popped them out of their prickly shells, have a great trick of hiding under the leaves.

"Oh, I've found one!" cried Nan. "Two—three! Oh, Bert, I've found three!" She held out her hand with three shining brown nuts in it.

"Ought to be a lot more than that here," said Bert, still poking away among the leaves. "There's lots of trees and fresh burrs here. I guess the squirrels and chipmunks have been here too."

"Oh, I've found two more! I'm beating you!" laughed Nan, as she picked up more nuts.

"I've found one, anyhow, and it's a big one," cried Bert, as he picked up his first. "But there aren't as many as I thought there would be."

The children continued to pick up a few nuts at a time, but there were not so many scattered over the ground as the lumberman had led them to expect.

"There's the chap who's been taking the nuts!" suddenly cried Bert.

"Who?" asked Nan, looking up after stooping to pick two of the brown prizes from a bursted burr.

"That squirrel!" cried Bert, pointing to one of the big-tailed gray fellows, sitting on a tree and looking down at the Bobbsey twins. "He and the chipmunks can soon clean up a chestnut grove."

Just then a red squirrel, one of the most noisy chatterers of the woods, caught sight of the children and began to "scold" them. Oh, what a racket he made, his thin tail jerking from side to side as he gave his shrill cries! Bert and Nan laughed at him.

"He's had his share of nuts," said Bert, "and he's mad 'cause we're taking some, I guess. But we aren't getting as many as we'd like."

"No," agreed Nan. "Maybe if we go on a little farther we'll find more."

"We'll try," agreed Bert and, almost before they knew it, the two children had wandered some distance from the place where Mr. Denton had told them to stop.

"Oh, look! There's a pile of nuts here!" cried Nan, reaching another grove of chestnut trees. "The squirrels haven't been here yet! Goodie!"

This was evident, for it did not take long, poking among the dried leaves, to show that the chestnuts were quite thick on the ground. In a short time Bert and Nan had half filled the salt bags they had brought with them to hold their spoils of the woods.

"Oh, this is great!" cried Nan, straightening up after four or five minutes of picking nuts from the ground.

"A little more of this and we'll have enough," said her brother.

But just then Nan looked up at the sky, which she could see through the overhead trees, and what she saw in the heavens made her exclaim:

"Bert, I believe it's going to storm! Look at the clouds! And it's getting ever so much colder, too!"

Indeed there was a chill in the air that had not been present when the Bobbsey twins started out that morning.

"Well, we'll go back in a few minutes," Bert suggested. But a little while after he had said this, there was a quick darkening of the air, the wind began to blow, and, so suddenly as to startle the children, they found themselves enveloped in such a blinding, driving squall of snow that they could not see ten feet on either side!

"Oh, Bert!" cried Nan. "It's a blizzard! Oh, shall we ever get back to Cedar Camp and to mother?"

Old Mrs. Bimby

"Pooh!" exclaimed Bert Bobbsey, as he ran through the half-blinding snowstorm toward Nan. "This isn't anything! It's only what they call a squall. I s'pose they call it that because the wind howls, or squalls, like a baby. Anyhow, I'm not afraid! It's fun, I think!"

By this time he had reached Nan's side, the two having been separated when the sudden storm burst. And now that Nan saw Bert near her and noticed that he had his bag of lunch, as she had hers, she took heart and said:

"Well, maybe it won't be so bad if we can find a place to stay, and can eat our dinner."

"Of course we can!" cried Bert. "There's lots of places to stay in these woods. We can find a hollow tree! I'll look for one!"

"Oh, don't!" cried Nan, as Bert moved away from her. "I don't want to go into a hollow tree. There might be owls in 'em!"

"Well, that's so," admitted Bert. "I'm not afraid of owls," he said quickly, "but of course their claws could get tangled in your hair. I'll look for another place—or I can make a lean-to. That's what the lumbermen and hunters do."

"I think it would be just as easy to get under one of the big, green Christmas trees," suggested Nan. "Look, hardly any snow falls under them."

She pointed to a large cedar tree near them, and, as you may have noticed if you were ever in the woods where these trees grow, scarcely any snow drifts under their low-hanging branches.

"That would be a regular tent for us," said Nan.

"Yes," agreed Bert, peering through the storm at the tree toward which his sister pointed. "We could get under one of those. But I think maybe we'd better not stand still. Let's walk on."

"But toward home!" suggested Nan. "We oughtn't to go any farther gathering nuts, Bert."

"No, I guess not," he agreed. "Anyhow, we have quite a lot. We'll start back for Cedar Camp. And when we get hungry we'll stop under a Christmas tree and eat. I'm beginning to feel hungry now," and Bert felt in his overcoat pocket to make sure that the lunch, which he had put there, was still safe. It was, he was glad to find, and Nan had hers.

"Yes, we'll eat in a little while," she said. "But we'd better start back to camp."

So the two older Bobbsey twins started off in the blinding snowstorm, little realizing that they were going directly away from camp instead of toward it. The wind whipped the snow into their faces, so that they could see only a little way in advance. And as they were in a strange woods, with only a small path leading back to camp, it is no wonder they became lost.

But we must not forget that we have left Flossie and Freddie, the smaller Bobbsey twins, in trouble. In playing sawmill Freddie had tipped Flossie out of the wheelbarrow, and the little girl had rolled down the slippery pine-needle hill into the stream just above the dam.

"Come quick! Come quick!" Freddie had cried. "Flossie'll go over the waterfall! Oh, hurry, somebody!"

He knew enough about waterfalls to understand that they were dangerous; that once a boat or a person got into the current above the falls they would be pulled along, and cast over, to drop on the rocks below.

Poor Flossie was too frightened to cry. Besides, as she fell in her head went under the water, and you can't call out when that happens. Flossie could only gurgle.

Luckily, however, there were several lumbermen on the bank of the stream, floating the logs down to be snaked out by the hook and chain, and sawed into boards. One of these men, Jake Peterson, was nearest to Flossie when the little girl tumbled into the stream.

"I'll get you out!" cried Mr. Peterson.

He dropped the big iron-pointed pole with which he was pushing logs and ran toward the little girl, while Freddie, trying to do all he could, slid down the slippery hill, as it was a quicker way down than by running.

Into the water with his big rubber boots waded Mr. Peterson, and it was not a quarter of a minute after Flossie had fallen in before she was lifted out.

"Oh! Oh!" she managed to gasp and gurgle, as she caught her breath, after swallowing some of the ice-cold water. "Oh, am I dr-dr-drowned?"

"I should say not!" answered Mr. Peterson. "You'll be all right. I'll take you to mother."

By this time Mrs. Bobbsey and Mrs. Baxter had rushed out of the log cabin, and Tom Case came from his sawmill. Several other lumbermen, hearing Freddie's excited cries, came running up, but there was nothing for them to do, as Flossie was already rescued.

"What has happened?" cried Mrs. Bobbsey, as she saw her little girl, dripping wet, in the arms of Mr. Peterson.

"She fell in," explained the lumberman. "She wasn't in more than a few seconds, though. All she needs is dry clothes!"

"I—I dumped her in!" sobbed Freddie. "But I didn't mean to. We were playin' sawmill with the wheelbarrow, and I gave Flossie a ride, an' I slipped on the pine needles, and she rolled down the hill."

"Never mind, dear! You didn't mean to," answered his mother, soothingly. "We must get Flossie to bed and keep her warm so she won't take cold."

With Mrs. Baxter's help, this was soon done, and in a short time after the accident Flossie was sitting up in a warm bed, sipping hot lemonade and eating crackers, while Freddie sat near her, doing the same.

Unless Flossie caught cold there would be no serious results from the accident. But Mrs. Bobbsey used it as a lesson for Freddie, telling him always to be careful when on a pine-needle-covered hill, near the water especially.

Flossie was enjoying her importance now, and she was begging her mother to tell her a story, in which request Freddie joined, when Mrs. Bobbsey, looking out of the window, was surprised to see how dark the clouds had become all of a sudden.

"I believe we are going to have a snowstorm," she said. And a few minutes later the snow came down so thick and fast that the lumbermen had to stop work, because they could not see where to drive the horses, nor to guide the logs down the stream to the mill.

"My, what a storm!" exclaimed Mrs. Bobbsey, as she went to the window to look out. "A regular blizzard!"

"We can have fun coasting down hill!" laughed Freddie. "And Flossie can be out to-morrow, can't she, Mother?"

"Yes, I think so," answered Mrs. Bobbsey, hardly thinking of what she was saying. "I hope Bert and Nan started back from the chestnut grove before this storm broke," she said. "If they are out in this it will be dreadful! I must see if daddy has come back," she added, for her husband had gone to see about the missing Christmas trees. "If Bert and Nan are out in this storm they will lose their way, I'm sure."

And this is just what Bert and Nan did. Clutching their bundles of lunch, and with their bags of chestnuts in their hands, the two older Bobbsey twins were struggling onward through the storm. They were warmly dressed, and it was not as cold as weather they had often been out in before. But they had seldom been out in a worse storm.

"Hadn't we—maybe we'd better stop and rest and eat something, Bert," suggested Nan, after a while.

"Maybe we had," he agreed, half out of breath because it was hard work walking uphill and against the wind. And almost before they knew it the children were going up a hill, though they did not remember having come down one on their trip to the chestnut grove.

They found a sheltered place under a big cedar tree, and, crawling beneath its protecting branches, they sat on the bare ground, where there was, as yet, no snow. The white flakes swirled and drifted all about them, but the thick branches of the tree, growing low down, made a place like a green tent.

"It's nice in here," said Bert, as he opened his bundle of lunch.

"Yes, but we ought to be at home," said Nan.

"We'll go home as soon as we eat a little," said her brother.

But after they had each eaten a sandwich and some cookies, and Bert had cracked a few chestnuts between his teeth and had found them rather too cold and raw to be good, the twins decided to go on.

Out into the storm they went, away from the shelter of the friendly tree. The storm was worse, if anything, and, without knowing it, Bert and Nan had become completely turned around. Every step they took carried them farther and farther away from their home camp. And they had journeyed quite a distance from the cabin before finding any chestnuts.

"Oh, Bert!" Nan exclaimed after a while, half sobbing, "I can't go a step farther. The snow is so thick, and it's so hard to walk in. And the wind blows it in my face, and I'm cold! I can't go another step!"

"That's too bad!" Bert exclaimed. "Maybe we're almost back to camp, Nan."

"It doesn't look so," his sister answered, trying to peer about through the swirling flakes.

"Wait a minute!" suddenly cried Bert, as there came a lull in the blast of wind. "I think I see something—a cabin or a house."

"Maybe it's our cabin," suggested Nan, "though I don't remember any of the trees around here. There aren't any cut down here as there are in camp."

"Well, I see something, anyhow," and Bert pointed to the left, off through the driving flakes. "Let's go there, Nan."

Through the storm the children struggled, hand in hand. They reached a log cabin—a lonely log cabin it was, standing all by itself in the midst of a little clearing in the woods.

"This isn't our camp, Bert!" said Nan.

"No," the boy admitted. "But somebody lives here. I see smoke coming from the chimney. I'm going to knock."

With chilled fingers Bert pounded on the cabin door.

"Who's there?" asked a woman's voice above the racket of the storm.

"Two of the Bobbsey twins!" answered Nan, not stopping to think that everyone might not know her and her brother by this name.

"Please let us in!" begged Bert. "We're from Cedar Camp! Who are you?"

"I'm Mrs. Bimby," was the answer, but neither Bert nor Nan recognized the name. A moment later the cabin door was opened, and an old woman confronted them. She looked at the two children for a moment; then, "Did you bring any news of Jim?" she asked.

Mr. Bobbsey Is Worried

Bert and Nan Bobbsey stood on the step of the log cabin, while Mrs. Bimby, the old woman, held open the door. The snow blew swirling in around her, and a wave of grateful warmth seemed to rush out as if to wrap itself around the cold twins. For a moment they stood there, and Bert was just beginning to wonder if the old woman was going to shut the door in the faces of his sister and himself.

"Did you bring any news of Jim?" asked old Mrs. Bimby.

"Jim?" repeated Bert.

"Do you mean Jim Denton, the foreman at Cedar Camp?" asked Nan.

"No, child! I mean my Jim—Jim Bimby. He went off to town just before this awful storm. But land sakes! here I am talking and keeping you out in the cold. Come in!"

It was cold. Bert and Nan were beginning to feel that now, for the storm was growing worse, and it was now late afternoon. The sun was beginning to go down, though of course it could not be seen on account of the snow and clouds. The Bobbsey twins had wandered farther and longer than they had thought. But at last they had found a place of shelter.

"It's just like me to keep you standing there while I talk," said Mrs. Bimby. "I'm sorry. But I'm so worried about Jim that I reckon I don't know what I'm doing. Come in and get warm, and I'll give you something to eat."

"We've got something to eat, thank you," said Nan. "But we would like to get warm," and she followed Bert inside the log cabin, as Mrs. Bimby stepped aside to make room for them to enter.

"Got something to eat, have you?" questioned the old woman. "Well, you're lucky, that's all I've got to say. I've only a little, but I expect Jim back any minute with more, though a dollar don't buy an awful lot these days."

"Does Jim live here?" asked Bert, as he walked over to a stove, in which a fire of wood was burning, sending out a grateful heat.

"Of course he lives here," said Mrs. Bimby. "He's my husband. He's a logger—a lumberman."

"Oh, maybe he works for my father!" exclaimed Nan. "Mr. Bobbsey, you know. He owns part of Cedar Camp."

"No, I don't know him," said Mrs. Bimby, "though I've heard of Cedar Camp. They got a lot of Christmas trees out of there."

"That's what we came up about," explained Bert. "Some Christmas trees my father bought to sell didn't come to Lakeport, and he came up here to see about them. We came with him—and my mother and the other twins."

"Good land! are there more of you?" asked Mrs. Bimby in surprise. "You two are twins, for a fact. But—"

"There's Flossie and Freddie," interrupted Nan. "We left them back in camp while we went after chestnuts."

"We got some, too," added Bert. "But we sort of got lost in the storm. Do you s'pose your husband could take us back to Cedar Camp?" he asked Mrs. Bimby. "My father will pay him," he said, quickly, as he saw Mrs. Bimby shaking her head.

"Maybe Mr. Bimby works at the sawmill," suggested Nan.

"No," said the old woman, "Jim is a logger and wood cutter, but he doesn't work at Cedar Camp. That's too far off for him to go to and get back from."

"Too far off!" echoed Nan, and she began to have a funny feeling, as she told Bert afterward.

"Yes," resumed Mrs. Bimby. "Cedar Camp is away over on the other side of the hills. You're a long way from home. You must have taken the wrong road in the storm."

"I—I guess we did," admitted Bert. "But couldn't your husband take us back?"

Again Mrs. Bimby shook her head.

"Jim, my husband, isn't home," she said. "He went over to town just before the storm to get us something to eat. But now I don't see how he's going to get back," and she went to a window to look out at the storm.

It was getting much worse, as Bert and Nan could see. The wind howled around the corners of the log cabin of Jim Bimby, the logger, and the blast whistled down the chimney, even blowing sparks out around the door of the wood-burning stove.

"Yes, it's a bad storm," went on the old woman. "I wish Jim was back, and with some victuals to eat. When you twins knocked I thought it was Jim. I wish he'd come back, but he's an old man, and he may fall down in the snow and not be able to get up. He isn't as strong as he used to be. I'm certainly worried about Jim!"

"Oh, maybe he'll come along all right," said Nan, trying to be helpful and comforting.

"If he doesn't pretty soon it'll be night, and in all this storm he never can find his way after dark. But you children take your things off and sit up and have a cup of tea with me. I've got some tea and condensed milk left, anyhow."

"We can't take tea unless it's very weak," said Nan, remembering her mother's rule in this respect.

"All right, dearie, I'll make it weak for you twins, though I like it strong myself," said Mrs. Bimby. "My, what a storm! *What* a storm!" and she drew her shawl more closely around her shoulders as the wind howled down the chimney.

Bert and Nan took off their warm things, laying their packages of lunch and the bags of chestnuts on the table. Nan saw the old woman go to a closet, and the glimpse the Bobbsey girl had of the shelves showed her that they contained only a little food.

"Bert and I have some of our lunch left," said Nan.

"And you can have some, if you want to," went on Bert. "We put up a pretty good lunch, and there's more'n half of it left."

"Bless your hearts, my dears," said Mrs. Bimby. "I wouldn't take your lunch. You'll need it yourselves. I've a little victuals left in the house, though if my Jim doesn't get back soon there won't be much for to-morrow. My, what a storm! What a storm!"

The small log cabin seemed to shake and tremble in the wind, as though it would blow away. And the snow was now coming down so thickly that Bert and Nan could see only a short distance out of the window. There was little to see, anyhow, save trees and bushes, and these were fast becoming covered with snow.

Mrs. Bimby busied herself about the stove, putting the kettle on so she could make tea, and Bert and Nan watched her. The Bobbsey twins were wondering what would happen, how they could get home, and whether or not their father and mother would worry. Nan looked about the cabin. She did not see any beds, but a steep flight of stairs, leading up to what seemed to be a second story, might provide bedrooms, Nan thought. The cabin was clean and neat, and she was glad of that.

"I do hope Jim comes," murmured Mrs. Bimby, as she poured the boiling water on the dry tea leaves in the pot. "I do hope he isn't storm-bound!"

Bert and Nan hoped the same thing, for, somehow, Bert thought if Mr. Bimby came along he would take the twins back to Cedar Camp.

"Now sit up, dearies, and have some weak tea, and I'll take mine strong. I need it for my nerves," said the old woman.

And while Bert and Nan had thus found shelter from what turned out to be one of the worst storms ever remembered in the country around Cedar Camp, the other Bobbsey twins, Flossie and Freddie, were safe at home with their mother. Flossie was now cozy and warm after her dip into the water.

"There's your father!" exclaimed Mrs. Bobbsey, as she heard someone stamping off the snow at the front door. "I hope he has Bert and Nan with him."

But when Mr. Bobbsey came in alone and heard that the older twins had not come back from their nutting trip, a worried look came over his face.

"Not back yet!" he exclaimed. "Why, it's getting dark and the storm is growing worse! I must start out after them with some of the lumbermen. They must be lost!"

Old Jim

"Don't you think Bert and Nan will be along in a little while?" asked Mrs. Bobbsey of her husband, as she crossed the big front room in the log cabin to meet him.

"Be in *soon!*" he exclaimed. "Why, they've been gone too long now, and—"

Mrs. Bobbsey, not letting Flossie and Freddie see her, made a motion with her hands toward her husband. Then he understood that his wife did not want him to frighten the smaller twins by letting it become known how worried he was about Bert and Nan.

"Oh—yes," said Mr. Bobbsey, as he understood his wife's idea. "Oh, yes, Bert and Nan will be along soon now."

"I'll be glad!" exclaimed Freddie.

"So will I," added Flossie, from her place on one of the bunks in a bedroom opening out of the living room. "I want some chestnuts."

"Hello, little Fat Fairy! what's the matter with you?" asked her father, noticing for the first time that Flossie was in bed. "Sick?" he asked.

"I just fell in the water," Flossie explained.

"I dumped her in, but I didn't mean to," Freddie said.

"Oh! Up to some of your fireman tricks, were you?" laughed Mr. Bobbsey, for he saw, by a glance at his wife, that the small twins were now in no danger.

"No, Daddy, I wasn't playing fireman," Freddie answered, though that was one of his favorite pastimes. "We were going to make a sawmill."

"Oh!" exclaimed Mr. Bobbsey. "Well, whatever you do, keep away from the big buzz saw," he warned. "And now," he went on in a low voice to his wife, so Freddie and Flossie would not hear, "we must do something about Bert and Nan."

"Yes," she agreed. "I'm worried about them, but I didn't want Flossie and Freddie to know. Oh, to think of their being out in this storm!"

"It is pretty bad," her husband admitted. "I was caught in it, and hurried back. I didn't think the children would go far away."

"Nor I," said Mrs. Bobbsey. "I suppose they didn't find chestnuts where they expected to, and wandered on. Are there any wild animals in the woods?"

"Well, no, none to speak of," her husband said slowly. "You don't need to worry about that. But I'll get Jim Denton, and some of the men, and we'll start right out after Bert and Nan."

"I wish I could come with you!" exclaimed his wife, as anxious and worried as was Mr. Bobbsey.

"You'll have to stay here with Flossie and Freddie," he said. "I'll soon find Bert and Nan and bring them back."

"I hope so," murmured his wife, but as she glanced out of the window and saw how dark it was getting and how fast the snow still came down and heard how the wind howled, it is no wonder the mother of the older Bobbsey twins was worried. So was Mr. Bobbsey.

"I'll go right away and get Jim and some of the men, and we'll start out on the search," said Mr. Bobbsey, having warmed himself at the stove. "We must not wait!"

"No," agreed Mrs. Bobbsey. "I'll stay and amuse Flossie and Freddie."

The smaller Bobbsey twins, of course, did not worry because Bert and Nan had not yet come home. Flossie and Freddie were having too much fun playing a little game on the foot of Flossie's bed. Mrs. Baxter, the housekeeper, had started the game for the children by bringing in some funny wooden blocks her husband had cut out on one of the long winter evenings that were sometimes so dreary in Cedar Camp.

The blocks could be fitted together to make a house, a bridge, a boat and many other play objects, and Flossie and Freddie enjoyed playing with them, for which their mother was glad. She really was so worried that she could not very well talk to them or tell them stories.

Telling his wife to keep up her courage and not to worry too much, Mr. Bobbsey went out into the storm again.

"Where is daddy going?" asked Flossie, hearing the door shut.

"He's going to bring back Bert and Nan—and the chestnuts," said Mrs. Bobbsey, quickly. She knew the smaller twins would think more of the chestnuts than anything else, just at present.

"Oh, I like chestnuts!" cried Freddie. "I'm going to boast 'em an' roil 'em!" he exclaimed.

"Listen to him, Mother!" laughed Flossie. "He said 'boast an' roil,' an' he meant roast an' boil 'em, didn't he?"

"I think he did," said Mrs. Bobbsey, trying not to let the small twins see how worried she was.

"Oh, Freddie Bobbsey, look what you did!" suddenly cried Flossie. "You knocked over my steamboat!" For Freddie had toppled over the pile of blocks that Flossie had erected on the foot of her bed.

"Never mind. He didn't mean to," said Mrs. Bobbsey. "You can make another boat, Flossie."

"An' I'll help," offered Freddie.

Thus the two smaller Bobbsey twins amused themselves, with little thought of Bert and Nan except, perhaps, to wonder when they would come home with the chestnuts.

Meanwhile Mr. Bobbsey hurried through the fast-gathering darkness and the storm to the cabin of Jim Denton. Like the other men in the Christmas tree and lumber camp, the foreman had stopped work when the storm came with such blinding snow and a wind that turned bitter cold toward night.

"What's that?" cried Jim Denton, when Mr. Bobbsey called at his cabin. "Bert and Nan not back from chestnutting yet? Why, I s'posed they were back hours ago!"

"So did I, and I wish they were," said Mr. Bobbsey.

"Oh, shucks now! don't worry," said the jolly foreman. "We'll find 'em all right. We'll start right out."

He put on his big boots and warm coat and went with Mr. Bobbsey to the cabins of some of the lumbermen. Soon a searching party was organized, and away they started through the storm along the path that earlier in the day Bert and Nan had taken to go to the chestnut grove.

"They took their lunch with them," said Mr. Bobbsey, "so they wouldn't be hungry until now. But they may be lost or have fallen into some hole and be half snowed over."

"Or they may have found some logger's or hunter's cabin, and have gone in," said Jim Denton. "There are plenty of cabins scattered through these woods."

"I hope they have found shelter," said Mr. Bobbsey anxiously.

On through the storm went the father of the Bobbsey twins and his lumbermen searchers. They stopped now and then and shouted, but no answers came back.

They had been out about an hour, and had gone more than a mile along the path that it was supposed Bert and Nan had taken, when one of the men called:

"Wait a minute! I think I heard someone call."

They all stopped and listened. Above the blowing of the wind and the swishing of the fast-falling snowflakes, a faint and far-off voice could be heard.

"Help! Help!" it called.

"There they are!" shouted one of the lumbermen.

"That doesn't sound like either Bert or Nan," said Mr. Bobbsey. "But it may be someone who started to bring them back to camp and he, too, became lost."

They all listened again, and once more came the call, but still faint and far away.

"Help! Help!"

"It's over here!" cried Jim Denton. "Over to the right!"

Through the storm and darkness the rescue party hurried, sending out calls to tell that they were on the way. Now and again they heard the cry in answer, and it sounded nearer now.

At last Mr. Bobbsey saw a dark figure huddled in a heap near a pile of snow, which had drifted around a large rock.

"Here's someone!" cried Mr. Bobbsey.

A moment later he and the lumbermen were standing over the figure of a man, partly buried in the snow.

"Why, it's Jim! Old Jim Bimby!" exclaimed Jim Denton. "I know him. He lives several miles from here. He must have been lost in the storm, too. Jim! Jim!" he cried. "What you doing here?"

"I—I started to town for victuals," said old Jim Bimby, in faint tones. "The storm was too much for me. I was about giving up."

"We heard you call," said Tom Case.

"Did you see anything of two small children?" eagerly asked Mr. Bobbsey. "Twins, a boy and a girl! Did you see them?"

Anxiously he bent over to catch the old logger's answer.

Snowed in

Having been out in the cold and storm so long, Jim Bimby seemed to have become half frozen. He did not appear to understand what Mr. Bobbsey asked him. The old logger staggered to his feet, helped by some of the men from Cedar Camp, and looked about him.

"What's the matter?" asked Old Jim in a faint voice. "Did something happen? I remember startin' off to get—to get something to eat for my wife and me. Then I fell down, tired out, I guess."

"I guess you did!" exclaimed Tom Case. "And if we hadn't found you, you'd have been done for. We must get you to shelter."

"Take him around behind this big pine tree a minute," suggested Jim Denton. "He'll be out of the wind there, and we can give him a drink of the hot tea we brought along."

Some hot tea, mixed with milk, had been put in a thermos bottle and taken with the party to have ready for Nan and Bert, should the Bobbsey twins be found. Now this hot drink would do for poor old Jim Bimby.

Some of the men managed to light lanterns they carried, though it was hard work on account of the wind and snow, and the whole party, including the rescued man, went to the side of the big pine tree, which kept off some of the storm.

"There! I feel better," said Old Jim, as he swallowed the warm drink.

"And now can you tell us whether or not you saw my two children, Nan and Bert—the Bobbsey twins?" again asked their father anxiously.

Old Jim shook his head.

"No," he answered. "I didn't see any children. I came straight from my cabin, over the hill trail, to go to the village to get some food. The cupboard is almost bare at my house. I didn't think it was goin' to storm, and I was all taken aback when it did. I kept on, but I must have lost my way."

"Guess you did," said Mr. Peterson. "And you're not likely to get back on it in this storm, either."

"What!" cried Old Jim. "You mean to say I can't keep on to the store and take some food back to my wife?"

"Not in this storm!" said Tom Case. "You're miles from the store now, and more miles from your cabin. You'd best come to Cedar Camp with us, and in the morning, when the storm is over, you can go on again. Your wife has enough food to last until morning, hasn't she?"

"Yes, I guess so," answered Mr. Bimby.

"But what has become of Bert and Nan?" asked Mr. Bobbsey.

"Now look here, Mr. Bobbsey," said Tom Case, "don't go to worrying about those children. They're all right. Bert and Nan are smart, and when they saw this storm coming on they went to some shelter, you can depend on that. They'd know better than to try to make their way back to camp."

"Well, perhaps they would," admitted the father of the missing twins. "And perhaps, when we get back to camp, we'll find them there. Some logger or hunter may have found them and taken them to our cabin."

"Of course," agreed Mr. Peterson.

By this time "Old Jim," as he was called, to distinguish him from Jim Denton, the lumber foreman, was feeling much better. He was still weak, and he leaned on the arm of one of the lumbermen as they turned back. The storm was still fierce, and it was now night, but lanterns gave light enough to see the way through the forest.

Had it not been that the lumber and Christmas tree men knew their way through the woods, the party might never have reached Cedar Camp. As it was they lost the trail once, and had hard work to find it again. But finally they plunged through several drifts of snow that had formed, and broke out into the clearing around the sawmill.

"Did you find them?" cried Mrs. Bobbsey, when her husband came to the cabin, knocking the snow off his feet.

"No," he answered, and he tried to make his voice as cheerful as possible. "We didn't find them, but they're all right. They were probably taken in by some hunter or logger."

Even as he said this Mr. Bobbsey was disappointed that Bert and Nan had not been brought back to camp during his absence, for he had half hoped that he would find them there on his own return.

"Oh, I do hope they're all right!" said Mrs. Bobbsey.

"Of course they are!" her husband told her. "They'll be here in the morning."

"With chestnuts?" asked Flossie, who, with Freddie, had been awakened from an early evening sleep by the return of their father.

"Yes, they'll bring chestnuts," replied Mr. Bobbsey, trying to smile, though it was hard work, for he was really very much worried, as was his wife.

However, they did not let Flossie and Freddie know this. And as Mr. Bobbsey ate the warm supper which Mrs. Baxter set out for him, he told about the finding of Mr. Bimby, who had been taken to the cabin of Tom Case, there to spend the night.

"Can we see him?" cried Flossie, who did not seem any the worse for having fallen into the water.

"Maybe he can tell us a story about a real bear," added Freddie, for he had been rather disappointed, since coming to Cedar Camp, because no one could tell him where to find a bear.

"Maybe he can," said his father. "You shall see Old Jim, as the boys call him, in the morning."

Mr. and Mrs. Bobbsey did not pass a very happy night. They were much worried about the missing Nan and Bert, and though he tried to sleep, after Flossie and Freddie had gone to Slumberland, Mr. Bobbsey found it hard work. So did his wife.

More than once during the night, as they awakened after fitful naps and heard the wind howling around the cabin and the snow rattling against the windows, one or the other would say:

"Oh, I hope Bert and Nan are all right!"

And the other would say:

"I hope so!"

Morning came at last, but it was not such a morning as all in Cedar Camp had hoped for. They had expected the storm to be over, so that a searching party could again set out to find Bert and Nan.

But instead of the storm being over, it was even worse than the night before. A regular blizzard had set in, the snow coming out of the north on the wings of a cold wind. Great drifts were piled high here and there through the camp clearing, and when Freddie and Flossie looked from the window they could hardly see the sawmill.

"Oh, oh!" squealed Freddie. "Look, Flossie! Just look!"

"We're snowed in!" cried Flossie. "Oh, what fun we'll have!"

"It's just like Snow Lodge!" added Freddie, remembering a time spent there, when several adventurous happenings had taken place.

"Yes, I'm afraid we are snowed in," said Mr. Bobbsey, with an anxious look out of the window. "But I hope it will not last long. Well, here come Tom Case and Old Jim. I must see what they want," and he went to the door to let them in.

Meanwhile the snow came down steadily, and as Flossie had said, that part of the Bobbsey family at Cedar Camp was fairly snowed in. As for the other members of the family, Bert and Nan, we must now try to find out what had happened to them.

A Bare Cupboard

Having finished drinking the weak tea which Mrs. Bimby brewed for them, eating with it some of the lunch they had brought along, Bert and Nan sat in the lonely cabin in the woods wondering what would happen next. There was no other cabin or house near them, and as they heard the wind howl down the chimney and moan around the corners, and heard the rattle of hard snow against the window, the older Bobbsey twins were glad they had found this shelter.

"Do you think we'll be able to start back soon, Mrs. Bimby?" asked Nan, as she helped the old woman clear the tea things off the table.

"Back where, dearie?"

"Back to our camp."

"Oh, not to-night, surely," said Mrs. Bimby. "You won't dare venture out in this storm. It's getting worse, and black night is coming on. You just stay here with me. I can make up beds for you, and I'll be glad to have you, since my Jim isn't coming back, I reckon."

"What do you think has become of him?" asked Bert, who was interested in looking at a gun that hung over the mantel.

"Well, I reckon he got to the village, but found the storm so bad he didn't dare to start back," answered Mrs. Bimby.

Of course she did not know what had happened to Old Jim any more than Jim knew that the older Bobbsey twins were in his own cabin.

"But Jim'll be here in the morning," said his wife. "And I do hope he'll bring in something to eat. If he doesn't—"

She did not finish what she started to say, and Nan asked:

"Will you starve, Mrs. Bimby?"

"Well, not exactly *starve*, for I s'pose a body could keep alive on tea and condensed milk for a while. But we'll be pretty hungry. There'll be three to feed instead of just one," the old woman went on.

"We've some food left," said Bert. "And we can cook our chestnuts. We got quite a few before the storm came."

"Bless your hearts, dearies!" exclaimed Mrs. Bimby. "You may be able to eat chestnuts, but *my* old teeth are too poor for that. But I dare say we'll get along somehow, even if the cupboard is almost bare. Don't you want to go to bed?"

"Oh, it's too early," objected Bert.

"Have you any games we could play?" asked Nan.

She and her brother were in the habit of playing simple games at home before going to bed, and it seemed natural to do it now. After the first shock of feeling that they were lost in the snow storm had passed, the Bobbsey twins were quite content. They felt that their father and mother must realize that they were safe.

"Games, dearie?" asked Mrs. Bimby. "Well, seems to me there's some dominoes around somewhere, and I did see a checker board the other day. Jim used to play 'em when the loggers came in. I'll see if I can dig 'em out."

She rummaged through an old chest and brought to light a box of battered dominoes. But as several were missing it was hard to play a good game with them. As for the checkers, the board was there but the pieces, or men, were not to be found.

"But you can take kernels of corn," said Mrs. Bimby. "I've often seen my Jim do that."

"Checker men have to be of different color," said Nan, "and corn is all one color, isn't it?"

"There are red ears," suggested Bert. "Don't you remember we saw some when we were in the country?"

"Oh, yes!" exclaimed Nan.

"That's what I was going to say," remarked Mrs. Bimby. "I can give you some yellow kernels and some red ones, and you can play checkers if you like."

This suited Nan and Bert, and though it was hard to make "kings" by placing one grain of corn on top of another, they managed to go on with the game, using pins to fasten two red or two yellow kernels one on top of the other when the king row was reached.

Grains of corn or some other cereal, or perhaps colored stones, were, very likely, the first sort of "men" used in the ancient game of checkers, and Bert and Nan got along very well in this way. Mrs. Bimby kept stoking the fire, putting on stick after stick of wood as it burned away, and the cabin was kept warm and cozy.

Outside the storm raged, the wind blew, and the snow came pelting down. But at times the older Bobbsey twins were so interested in their checker game that they hardly heard the sounds outside the log cabin.

At last Mrs. Bimby, with a look at the clock, said:

"It's after nine, dearies; hadn't you better go to bed? My Jim won't come to-night, that's sure, and I don't believe any of your folks will come for you."

"They don't know where we are," said Nan.

"No more they do, dearie. Well, I'll show you where you're to sleep. I'm glad I've got covers enough for two extra beds."

There were three rooms in the second story of the log cabin. Two of the rooms were small, each one containing a little single cot. The other room was larger, and had a bed in it. Mrs. Bimby slept there, and she gave Bert and Nan each one of the smaller rooms. There was a window in each of the bedrooms, and being above the warm downstairs room, where a hot fire had been blazing all evening, the sleeping chambers were more comfortable than one would have supposed.

Bert and Nan were so sleepy that they did not lie awake long after getting to bed. As there were no pajamas for Bert and no night-gown for Nan, the children slept in their underclothes, taking off only their shoes and outer garments.

In spite of the fact that he fell asleep soon after going to bed, because he was tired from the day's tramp after chestnuts, Bert was awakened in the middle of the night by hearing Nan call:

"Mother, please give me a drink!"

It was a request Bert had often heard his sister make before, and now he realized that she was either half awake, and did not remember where she was, or else she was talking in her sleep. He raised up on his elbow and listened. Again Nan said:

"I want a drink!"

Bert knew how hard it was to try to go to sleep when thirsty, so he got up and, having noticed on coming to bed the evening before a pail of water on a chair in the upper hall, he brought Nan a dipper full. Mrs. Bimby had left a lantern burning, so it was not dark in the cabin.

"Oh, Bert! I dreamed I was back home," said Nan, as she took the drink her brother handed her. "Thank you!"

"Welcome," he said, struggling to keep his sleepy eyes open.

"Is it still snowing?" asked Nan.

"Hard," answered Bert, looking out of the window, though, truth to tell, he could see nothing, it was so pitch dark outside. But he could hear the rattle of snow against the glass.

"I hope it stops by morning," sighed Nan.

"So do I—long enough for us to get back to camp, anyhow," added Bert.

He got himself a drink and went back to bed, there to sleep soundly until morning, when Mrs. Bimby called him and Nan to get up.

"Come, dearies," said the kind old woman. "We'll have breakfast, such as it is."

For a few moments after awakening Bert and Nan could not quite remember where they were. Bert afterward said that he hoped there would be hot buckwheat cakes for breakfast, with maple syrup, such as they had had in the cabin where Mrs. Baxter acted as cook. But there was no such appetizing smell as that of pancakes coming up from Mrs. Bimby's kitchen.

"I'm sorry I haven't any more to offer you," she said to the children, as she set before them some more weak tea and a few pieces of bread and butter. "If my Jim had come back we'd have had enough to eat. But as it is, I'm afraid you'll go hungry soon."

"We'll eat what's left of our lunch," said Bert.

"And cook some chestnuts," added Nan. "We'll pretend we've been shipwrecked. Were you ever shipwrecked, Mrs. Bimby?" Nan asked, as cheerfully as she could.

"No, dearie, but I've had the rheumatiz, and I reckon that's 'most as bad. But let's eat what we've got and we'll hope for more before the day is over."

"It's still snowing, isn't it?" remarked Nan, as she hungrily ate some of the dry food and swallowed some of the weak, but warm, tea.

"Yes, and it's likely to keep up all day," said Mrs. Bimby. "It'll be hip-deep by night, and we'll be completely snowed in. I declare, I don't know what we'll do!"

"Maybe it'll stop," suggested Bert, trying to look on the bright side.

"Or maybe it won't be so bad but what we can go out," added Nan. "And if we get back to camp we can send you something to eat by one of the men in a sleigh, Mrs. Bimby."

"I wouldn't let you go out in this storm—not for anything!" declared the kind old woman. "The only safe place is this cabin when it snows this way. You can't starve to death as quickly as you can freeze to death, that's a comfort. And we've got enough for one more meal, anyhow."

But when noon came, after a long morning, during which the Bobbsey twins played more checker games with grains of corn, and when almost all there was in the cupboard had been eaten, Mrs. Bimby opened the doors, looked at the bare shelves and said:

"I declare, I don't know what we're going to do! Almost everything is gone!"

The cupboard, indeed, was nearly bare.

For some reason or other, Bert's eyes rested on the gun on the wall over the mantel.

"Is that gun loaded, Mrs. Bimby?" he asked.

"Yes, I reckon 'tis," she answered. "Jim always keeps it loaded, for he goes hunting sometimes."

"What after?" asked Bert.

"Oh, squirrels and rabbits."

"That's what I'm going to do, then!" cried Bert. "If I could shoot some squirrels or rabbits we'd have a potpie and we wouldn't be hungry. Will you please get that gun down for me, Mrs. Bimby?"

She looked at Bert and smiled.

"You're pretty small to handle a gun," she said. "But maybe you could fire it if I showed you how. I've shot it more 'n once, and I brought down a cawing crow last winter. Sometimes the rabbits come close up to our cabin here. Wait till I take a look."

She went to the window to peer out into the storm, and Nan did likewise, while Bert continued to gaze at the gun on the wall. It was a shotgun, not very heavy, and he felt certain he could aim it at a rabbit and pull the trigger.

Mrs. Bimby shook her head as she turned away from her window.

"There's no game here," she said. "Guess we'll have to go without a potpie."

But Nan suddenly uttered an exclamation.

"Oh, I see one!" she cried. "I see a big rabbit! Two of 'em! Oh, Bert, it's a shame to shoot the bunnies, but we can't starve! Get the gun!"

Bert Starts out

Just about the time that Bert was getting ready to try for a rabbit potpie by firing the gun from the door of Mrs. Bimby's cabin, in the other and larger cabin at Cedar Camp the smaller Bobbsey twins were having a good time. There was no danger there of starving, for the cupboard was far from being bare.

But of course Mr. and Mrs. Bobbsey were worried because, after their long night of worry, neither Bert nor Nan had come back, and there was no news of them.

"But we'll surely hear from them to-day," said Tom Case, as he came over through the storm after breakfast to learn if Mr. Bobbsey had any special plans.

"How's Old Jim?" asked Mr. Bobbsey, as the head of the sawmill workers came in out of the storm, for it was still snowing.

"Oh, Jim's all right," was the answer. "But he's worrying about his wife not having any food. I came over to say that if the storm lets up a little maybe we'd better try to take something to eat to the old lady. She's all alone in her cabin."

Of course neither he nor Old Jim knew that the two older Bobbsey twins were at that very moment with Mrs. Bimby.

"All right, it would be a good idea," said Mr. Bobbsey. "And we must make another search for Bert and Nan."

"I have a sort of feeling that they're safe," said Mr. Case. "And, really, it wouldn't be wise for you to start out in this storm to look for them. I think it may moderate a little by to-morrow."

"Let us hope so!" sighed Mrs. Bobbsey.

"Can't Old Jim come over and play with us?" asked Flossie.

"We want to have some fun," added Freddie.

The two smaller twins had been as good as possible, but they were not used to being cooped up in the house, and there really was not much to do in the cabin. No toys had been brought along, for Mr. Bobbsey had not expected to stay very long in looking after his Christmas trees. And he certainly never counted on being snowed in.

"Yes, I'll bring Old Jim over," said Mr. Case. "He's pretty good at making things with his pocket knife. Shouldn't wonder but what he could cut you out a doll, Flossie."

"Can he make boats?" asked Freddie.

"Sure he can!" said the sawmill foreman.

"Where you going to sail a boat in the snow, Freddie Bobbsey?" asked Flossie.

"I—I'll have him make me a snow-boat!" the little fellow said.

"Pooh!" laughed Flossie. "There are ice-boats, 'cause we rode in one once, but there aren't any snow-boats, are there, Daddy?"

"Well, perhaps Old Jim can make one," her father said. "Bring him over, Tom. I want to talk to him and find out where would be the most likely place for Nan and Bert to have found shelter."

The old logger, who seemed to have gotten over his exposure to the storm, came to the Bobbsey cabin, and he somewhat relieved the worries of Bert's father and mother by saying there were a number of cabins of loggers and trappers scattered through the woods, and he had an idea that Bert and his sister might have reached one of these.

"Well, we'll start out and look for them as soon as the storm lets up a little," said Mr. Bobbsey.

Freddie and Flossie made great friends with Old Jim. They took to him at once, and when he cut out of a piece of wood a queer doll for Flossie, and made for Freddie a thin wooden wheel, which would turn around in the waves of heat arising from the hot stove, the children were delighted.

They climbed all over Old Jim, and laughed and shouted as though they had no cares in the world. And, as a matter of fact, they were not old enough to worry about Bert and Nan. They thought their older brother and sister would come along sooner or later.

Slowly the day of storm passed, but with no let-up in the falling snow. The wind, while it did not blow as violently as at first, was high and cold, so that the little Bobbsey twins could not go out.

And it was about the time that Flossie and Freddie were having such fun with Old Jim that, back in this same logger's lonely cabin, Bert and Nan were wondering whether they would have anything to eat for supper.

As Nan had said, she did see two large rabbits when she looked from the window. And she called to her brother to get the gun from its place over the mantel.

"Land sakes!" exclaimed Mrs. Bimby, "there *are* two right in plain sight. Now Bert, if you're any kind of a shot, maybe we'll have rabbit stew for supper. Here, take the gun, but be careful!"

Bert knew a little about firearms, and he was not at all afraid as Mrs. Bimby put the shotgun into his hands. Then she opened the door for him, very carefully, so as not to frighten the rabbits.

"They're still there, right on top of the snow!" called Nan, as she peered from the window on her side of the cabin. "I'm not going to watch you shoot them, Bert, though I am terribly hungry. And I'm going to hold my hands over my ears so I won't hear the gun."

Bert was quite excited, and did not pay much attention to what his sister was saying, but he was not so excited that he could not hold the gun fairly steady.

"Hold it close against your shoulder, then it won't kick so hard," Mrs. Bimby whispered in his ear, as she helped him get the shotgun in place, and pointed it for him out of the open door.

The rabbits were in plain sight now, two wild, gray bunnies, fat and plump. Bert took sight over the little point on the end of the gun. He held this sight as steadily as he could in line with one of the rabbits.

"Better shoot quick!" whispered Mrs. Bimby. "I think they see us and they'll scoot away in a minute!"

Bert gave a steady pull on the trigger, not a sudden pull, which is not the right way to shoot. A sudden pull spoils your aim.

"Bang!" went the shotgun.

"Oh!" screamed Nan, who, in spite of having held her hands over her ears, heard the report.

"I got one! I got one!" excitedly cried Bert, as he saw one of the bunnies lying on the snow. The other had scampered off.

"Yes, you did get one, child!" said Mrs. Bimby, as she ran out into the storm and came back with the game. "Now we shan't starve. I'll make a potpie."

This she did, stewing the rabbit with some dumplings she made from a little flour she had left in the bottom of the barrel. Bert and Nan thought nothing had ever tasted so good as that rabbit potpie.

"You'll be quite a hunter when you grow up," said Mrs. Bimby, when the meal was over. "You shot straight and true, Bert!"

"But you helped me," said the Bobbsey boy. "I couldn't have aimed the gun straight if you hadn't helped me."

"But I saw the rabbits, didn't I?" asked Nan.

"Yes, dearie, you surely did," said the kind old woman. "Now we shan't starve for a couple of days, anyhow."

"And then I can shoot more rabbits, or maybe some squirrels," Bert declared.

"I hope by that time the storm'll be over," remarked Mrs. Bimby, "and that my Jim will come back."

"Will he take us home, or bring our father here?" Nan questioned.

"I guess so," Mrs. Bimby answered.

But as the snow kept up all the remainder of that day, and as it was still storming hard when night came, there did not seem much chance of the two older Bobbsey twins being rescued.

Again Bert and Nan spent the night in the little rooms of the cabin, but they slept better this time, Nan not even awakening for a drink of water. And in the morning Bert looked from a window and cried:

"Hurray! The snow's stopping! I'm going to start out and go back to camp!"

"You are?" asked Nan. "Are you going to take me?"

"No," said Bert. "You'd better stay here. I'll go to camp and send daddy back in a sled for you. He can hitch a horse to one of the lumber sleds now that the snow is stopping, and he can ride you home. And if I find your husband I'll send him back with a lot of things to eat," he told Mrs. Bimby.

"I wish you would, dearie," said the old woman. "But are you really going to start out, Bert?"

"Yes'm! My father and mother will be worried about us. I can get to camp now, I'm sure, as the storm is almost over."

Mrs. Bimby, who, though not very wise, was kind, made him take a little lunch with him, packing up some cold boiled chestnuts and part of the cold rabbit meat. It was all there was.

"But maybe I'll get to camp before I have to eat," said Bert. "And I'll send back help to you."

So Bert started out, Mrs. Bimby showing him the direction he was to take. It was still snowing a little, but he hoped it would soon stop.

Trying Again

Though Flossie and Freddie had what they called "good times" in the log cabin at Cedar Camp, and though Old Jim played with them, making boats and dolls of wood, still the small Bobbsey twins wished for the time to come when they might go out of doors. They also began to wish for the return of Bert and Nan.

"When *will* they come, Mother?" Flossie asked over and over again.

"And bring us chestnuts!" teased Freddie.

"Oh, they'll come soon now," Mrs. Bobbsey said, as she looked out of the window at the flakes of snow, still falling, and listened to the whistle of the cold wind around the cabin.

And in her heart how very much Mrs. Bobbsey wished that Bert and Nan would come back soon! Mr. Bobbsey wished the same thing, and the only comfort the father and mother had in those worrisome days was the thought that their older twins *must* have found shelter somewhere in the woods.

Old Jim declared that this was so, as, likewise, did Tom Case and Jim Denton. But it was still storming too much for another searching party to set out and look for Nan and Bert. Those who searched might themselves become lost in the blizzard. For that is what the storm now was—a regular blizzard.

Mr. Bobbsey could do nothing toward searching for the lost shipment of Christmas trees. The lumbermen could not work at cutting down trees, floating or sledding them to the mill or carting them to the railroad. Even the sawmill was shut down, and all there was to do was to wait.

Flossie and Freddie were not used to staying in the house so long at a time. They wanted to go out and play even if there was snow, but their mother would not let them in such an unusual storm.

"It's like when we were at Snow Lodge," sighed Flossie, as she stood with her little nose pressed flat against the window, thereby making her face cold.

"We could go out a little there," sighed Freddie.

"I think you children are very lucky," said their mother. "You have a warm place to stay. Think of poor Nan and Bert. They may—"

She stopped suddenly. She dared not think of what her older son and daughter might be suffering. She glanced quickly at Flossie and Freddie. She was afraid lest she should make them worry, too.

But, fortunately, Flossie and Freddie were not that sort. They did not believe in worrying, unless it was over not having fun enough. However, the log cabin was of good size, and with Old Jim to come over now and then to amuse them with cutting out wooden toys, the two Bobbsey twins did not have such a sad time as might be imagined.

To-day, however, when the storm had kept up so long, and when they had not had a chance to go out, they felt rather lonesome and as if they wanted to "do something." So, presently, when Flossie had grown tired of pressing her nose against the glass, making it cold, and then holding it on Freddie's cheek to hear him exclaim in surprise, the little girl wandered about looking for something to do. Freddie joined her, and while their mother was in another room, talking to Mr. Bobbsey, and saying he ought, soon, to make another trip and search for Bert and Nan, Flossie and Freddie went up in the top story of the log cabin.

The log cabin was the largest in that part of the woods, and was higher than most, so that in addition to the bedrooms on the second floor, there was, above them, an open attic, reached by a short flight of steps, and in it were stored all sorts of odds and ends.

"Maybe we can find something here to play with," suggested Flossie.

"Maybe," agreed Freddie.

They rummaged around in the half-dark place, back in corners where the roof came down slanting and making little "cubby-holes," and it was after a glance into one of these places that Flossie drew back and whispered to Freddie:

"There's a bear in here!"

"A bear! Where?" and Freddie moved over closer to Flossie and looked where she pointed.

"There," said the little girl, and, glancing along the line of her outstretched finger, Freddie saw a big, furry heap in a dark corner. "I touched it first with my foot," said Flossie, "and it was soft, just like the bear I touched that the Italian had once, leading around by a string in his nose. And then I put out my hand and I felt his fur!"

"Oh!" exclaimed Freddie. "Did he—did he bite you?" He had been looking for something to play with on the other side of the attic, and, therefore, had not seen all that Flossie had.

"Course he didn't bite me!" the little girl answered. "You didn't hear me holler, did you?"

"No," said Freddie, "I didn't. I'm going to touch him!"

"Come over here," advised Flossie, moving to one side so Freddie could thrust his hand forward and touch that mysterious heap of fur. "I–I guess maybe he's asleep, that's why he didn't growl or nothin'!"

"I guess maybe," agreed Freddie. Neither of the Bobbsey twins felt surprised because they had an idea a bear might be in the attic with them. Nor were they afraid. A sleeping bear is not dangerous, of course. Any little boy or girl knows that!

Freddie crawled a little way farther under the sloping roof and, by stretching out his hand, managed to touch the fur. It felt warm and soft to his fingers.

"Oh, it is a bear!" he whispered, and he was delighted. "Let's go and tell mother, and we can bring it downstairs and play with it. I guess it's a little bear!"

"Yes, we'd better tell mother," agreed Flossie. Somehow, the more she thought of a bear being up in the attic the more she thought it better to have some of the older folks know about it.

Down the stairs went the two Bobbsey twins, walking softly so as not to awaken the bear. They didn't want him suddenly aroused from his sleep and made cross. Who would?

"Where have you children been?" cried Mrs. Bobbsey, as she saw the two twins. They were covered with dust and cobwebs from having crawled so far under the sloping roof in the attic. The floor was dirty, too, not having been swept in many months, and they had sat right down in the worst of the dust.

"Oh, Mother!" gasped Flossie, "we've been up in the attic, and what do you think's up there? It's a—"

"*Bear!*" burst out Freddie, not wanting his sister to tell all the wonderful news. "He's asleep, an' I touched him!"

"Nonsense!" exclaimed Mrs. Bobbsey. "A bear? It can't be!"

And yet she knew there were bears in the North Woods, and it might be possible that one had crawled into the cabin before they had come, and had gone to the attic to have his long winter sleep.

"Yes, it is a bear!" insisted Flossie, and both children were so certain about the heap of fur that Mrs. Bobbsey called her husband, who was out in the woodshed with Tom Case and Jim Bimby.

"A bear!" cried the mill foreman. "Well, there are some around these woods, but I never knew of one coming into a cabin. I'll take a look."

"Hadn't you better take a gun?" asked Mr. Bobbsey, as he and Old Jim followed the foreman upstairs. "There's one here."

"Well, you might hand it to me," said Mr. Case. "But I reckon if it is a bear that's crawled in to go to sleep, he'll be so lazy I can take him by the back of the neck and throw him out."

Freddie and Flossie waited with their mother while their father and the two men went to the attic. They could hear the three moving around up overhead, and soon there was a shout of laughter.

"Maybe it's a circus bear, and he's doing tricks!" exclaimed Flossie.

"Oh, I hope it is!" added Freddie, feeling quite excited.

Their father and the two men came downstairs. Tom Case carried something—something brown and shaggy, just like the fur of some animal.

"There's your 'bear!'" he said, laughing, as he tossed the furry object over a chair. "A bear skin! Ha! Ha!"

And that is what it was. The skin of a big bear, made into a lap robe for use in cold weather. The fur was warm, thick and soft, and when the skin was huddled up in a heap in a corner no wonder the Bobbsey twins mistook it for a real bear, especially in the dark.

"That's a good warm fur robe," said Old Jim. "If it was made into a fur coat it would keep out the cold."

"Maybe that's what the man who used to live here was going to use it for," said Mr. Bobbsey. "He moved away and forgot it. Well, you children can play with it," he said to Flossie and Freddie. "It was a bear once."

And the Bobbsey twins had fun taking turns wrapping the bear skin about them and pretending to be different kinds of wild animals.

It was when the storm began to grow less severe, the wind not blowing so hard and the snow not coming down so thickly, that Mr. Bobbsey, looking from the window when Flossie and Freddie were playing "bear," said:

"I think I'll start out again."

"Where?" asked his wife.

"To find Bert and Nan," he answered. "I think the blizzard is about over, and they will probably be starting for home. I'll go to meet them."

"Oh, take us!" cried Flossie and Freddie. "We want to see Bert and Nan."

"Oh, no, I couldn't take you," said their father. "The snow is piled deep in drifts, and you'd sink away down in—over your heads. I'll take some of the men and start," he said to his wife.

And so, a little later, another searching party started away from Cedar Camp to find the missing Bobbsey twins.

"I'll go along," said Old Jim, who was now able to travel. "I must take some food to my wife. She'll be 'most starved."

"Yes, come with us," said Mr. Bobbsey. "We'll take some food to Mrs. Bimby."

A Little Searching Party

Flossie and Freddie Bobbsey were two of the kindest children in the world. They were fond of fun and of having a good time, but whenever their mother did work for the church at home, helping poor families, taking food to people who had but little, Freddie and Flossie always wanted to do their share. So did Bert and Nan; but as the older twins had to spend more time in school than did Flossie and Freddie, the two latter had more chances to help their mother.

More than once they had gone with her when she carried a basket of food or a bundle of clothing to some poor family in Lakeport. And now, in Cedar Camp, having heard their father say he was going to take food to Mrs. Bimby, Flossie and Freddie at once had an idea.

While Mr. and Mrs. Bobbsey were out of the room, talking over the coming trip through the woods to look for Bert and Nan, as well as to take food to Mrs. Bimby, Freddie said to Flossie:

"Let's go, too!"

"Daddy won't let us," Flossie answered.

"We—we'll tag after him," said Freddie in a whisper. "We can put on our rubber boots and our coats and mittens, and we can go behind him. He can't hear us, 'cause there's so much snow our boots won't make any noise."

"That's so," agreed Flossie. "And, oh, Freddie! I know what we can do."

"What?"

"We can take Mrs. Bimby that bear robe. It'll keep her warm, 'cause it's so nice and soft!"

"So 'tis!" agreed Freddie. "We'll take it, and something to eat, too."

"We'll not have to do that, Daddy and the other men are going to take her something to eat."

"I meant something to eat for us," Freddie said. "We ought to take a lunch with us, 'cause maybe we'll get hungry in the woods."

The younger Bobbsey twins had a feeling that if they were seen packing up a lunch for themselves, putting on their boots and outdoor garments, and taking the bear skin, they would be stopped. They felt sure they would not be allowed to go in search of Nan and Bert. And they were probably right.

So, as they had done more than once before, they said nothing of their plans, but went about them secretly and quietly. While their mother and Mrs. Baxter were packing two large baskets with food for Old Jim's wife, and while Daddy Bobbsey was talking to the men about the coming trip through the snow-filled woods, Flossie and Freddie took their boots, coats, caps and mittens to the back door of the log cabin.

"We can slip out and put 'em on there when nobody is looking," said Freddie.

"We've got to take the bear skin out, too," Flossie remarked.

But when they tried to bundle the skin of the bear up so they could carry it, they found it so heavy and slippery to lift that they had to give it up.

"What'll we do?" asked Flossie, as, after several trials she had to admit that the skin could not be carried. "Mrs. Bimby'll be so disappointed!"

"We can tell her it's here, and Mr. Jim can come and get it," suggested Freddie.

"Oh, that'll be nice!" his sister agreed. "We'll leave the skin."

How to pack up a lunch for themselves was also a hard matter. But, as it happened, Mrs. Bobbsey was so busy getting things ready for her husband and the other men that she did not pay much attention to what Flossie and Freddie did. She saw them moving about, now in the pantry and now in the kitchen and again stepping to the back door, but she did not dream they were getting ready to set off on a search by themselves.

However, this is just what Flossie and Freddie were going to do, and, after a while, they managed to pack into a pasteboard box what they thought would be lunch enough for them until they came back with Bert and Nan.

"Put in lots of cake," whispered Freddie to Flossie, on one of the little girl's trips to the pantry. "Cake tastes awful good in the woods."

"I will," Flossie whispered back. "And I got some pie, too!"

"Oh, that's fine!" Freddie exclaimed. "Now we must slip out when they don't see us."

This the small Bobbsey twins managed to do. While Mr. Bobbsey, with Old Jim and Tom Case, was making ready to start on his searching expedition, to find and bring back Bert and Nan, as well as to take food to lonely Mrs. Bimby, Flossie and Freddie slipped quietly to the back door with their queer package of lunch.

They soon donned their boots, coats and caps, and with their little hands covered with warm, red mittens, they started off, keeping behind the cabin so they would not be seen by those in front who were getting ready to start on the main searching trip. It was snowing a little, but not nearly so hard as at first, and the wind was not so strong or cold.

"It'll be fun!" said Flossie to Freddie.

"Lots of fun!" agreed her twin. "We'll wait until daddy and Mr. Jim and Mr. Case get in the woods, and then we'll follow 'em. They won't send us back!"

"No," agreed Flossie, "I don't guess they will."

The plan of the little Bobbsey twins was to follow their father on the search. They did not want to go through the woods alone, even though it was now daylight, though the sun did not shine because of the snow clouds.

And so, a little while after Mr. Bobbsey and the two men started away from the log cabin, Flossie and Freddie set out on their own little searching party. Mrs. Bobbsey and Mrs. Baxter were so busy "cleaning up" after the men left that they gave no thought to the children for a time.

"There they go!" whispered Flossie to Freddie, as, hiding behind a woodpile, they saw their father, Mr. Bimby and Tom Case start off.

"Wait a little, and then we'll go after 'em," advised Freddie.

As soon as the main party had marched off along the trail that led through the woods toward the chestnut grove that Bert and Nan had set out to visit two days before, the small Bobbsey twins set forth. They went around behind a clump of trees so they would not be seen from the cabin.

Flossie and Freddie expected soon to catch up to their father, but the snow was so deep and the men traveled so fast that, after trudging along for half an hour, Freddie and his sister had not yet come within sight of the others.

"Do you s'pose they ran away from us?" asked Flossie, as she stopped a moment to rest.

"Course not," answered Freddie. "They don't even know we're comin' after 'em."

"That's so," Flossie said. "Well, anyhow, I hope we don't get lost."

"I do, too," agreed Freddie. "But we have something to eat, anyhow," and he patted the box of lunch he carried.

The children looked around them. They were in a lonely part of the woods, a place they had never been before, but they felt sure they would soon catch up to their father. They had been following the tracks in the snow left by the men who had gone to find Bert and Nan and take food to Mrs. Bimby.

Suddenly, however, there came a harder flurry of snow, and for a time Flossie and Freddie could not see very well. And when the little squall, as sudden storms are called, had passed, the two Bobbsey twins found they had wandered off to one side of the trail.

No longer could they see the footprints of their father and the others in the snow. They had nothing to guide them!

"Freddie! Look!" cried Flossie, "Where's the path?" She called her father's snow-track a "path."

"Why, it—it's gone!" Freddie had to admit.

And then, as the two little children stood in the lonely snow-filled woods, they heard, near a bush, a noise that made them suddenly afraid.

It was a growl that they heard!

The Wildcat

Bert Bobbsey started off bravely enough from the cabin of Mrs. Bimby to go for help for the old woman, so that food might be taken to her bare cupboard.

"And I'll have daddy bring a sled or something so Nan can ride home to camp on it," thought Bert, as he trudged along through the snow. "It's hard walking. I wish I had a pair of snowshoes."

He had started away from the lonely cabin, as I told you two chapters back. With him he took a little package of lunch, not very much, for he felt sure he would soon reach Cedar Camp by following the line of the brook, nor was there much to be got from Mrs. Bimby's bare cupboard. Even though much snow had fallen, Bert hoped the bed of the brook could be made out once he came to it. It lay some distance from the cabin, he thought.

The Bobbsey twin boy turned, after trudging a little way from the cabin, and waved his hand at Mrs. Bimby and Nan, who stood near a window watching him.

"Your brother is a brave little chap," said Mrs. Bimby. "I do hope he finds help and brings it back to us."

"I hope so, too; 'specially something for you to eat," said Nan.

"Oh, well, we've a little of the rabbit left yet," said the old woman. "But my tea is 'most gone, and I need it strong on account of my nerves. If it wasn't for my rheumatiz I'd put on my things and go with Bert. I'd take you along, though I fear it's going to snow more."

"I hope it doesn't before Bert gets back to camp," Nan said. "I shouldn't want him lost all alone."

"Nor I, dearie," crooned Mrs. Bimby. "But he's a brave lad, and I trust he gets along all right. Though it has been a bad storm—a bad storm!" she muttered.

She put more wood on the fire, for, though the wind had gone down a little and the snow was not falling so rapidly, it was still cold. But the blazing wood threw out a grateful heat, and Nan and Mrs. Bimby sat about the stove, waiting for the help Bert was to send.

Bert felt a little lonely as he plunged into the woods and lost sight of the cabin. Though it was daylight, and the woods were not dark because of the white snow, still Bert felt a little lonesome. He wished Nan had come with him.

"But I guess a girl couldn't get along," he said to himself, as he plunged through drift after drift. Indeed it was hard work for Bert, sturdy as he was, to wade along, especially as he had on no boots, not having expected a storm when he and Nan started after chestnuts.

"Now let me see," said Bert Bobbsey, talking to himself half aloud, to make his trip seem less lonesome. "The first thing I want to do is to find the brook. I can follow that back to camp, I'm pretty sure. But it's a good way from here, I guess."

He remembered having seen the brook just before he and Nan reached the first chestnut grove, where they found the squirrels and chipmunks had taken most of the supply, making the children go farther on. And then the Bobbsey twins had rather lost sight of the stream of water.

Bert knew it might be almost hidden from sight under overhanging banks of snow, but he knew if he could come upon the water course it would be the surest thing to follow to get back to camp. So as he trudged along, into and out of drifts, he looked eagerly about for a sign of the brook, which, as it went on, widened and ran into the mill pond near Cedar Camp.

Bert was all by himself in the snowy woods. The cabin, where his sister and Mrs. Bimby waited for him to bring help, was lost to sight amid the trees. For the first time since leaving Cedar Camp Bert began to feel lonesome and afraid.

It was so still and quiet in the woods! Not a sound! No birds fluttered through the trees or called aloud. The birds that had not flown south were, doubtless, keeping under shelter until they dared venture out to look for food, which some of them would never find.

"There isn't even a crow!" said Bert aloud, and his voice, in that white stillness, almost startled him by its loudness.

He reached the top of a little hill, where there was not quite so much snow, the wind having blown it off, and there Bert stopped for a moment, looking about. It was a lonesome and dreary scene that lay before him. Not a house in sight, only a stretch of snow and trees, and the wind howled mournfully through the bare, leafless branches.

"Well, there's no use standing here," murmured Bert to himself. "I've got to travel on and bring help to Nan and the old lady. I'm glad Nan has some shelter, anyhow. And I s'pose mother will be worrying about us. But we couldn't help it. Nobody would guess a storm would come up so quickly."

Throwing back his shoulders as he had seen men do when they had some hard task before them, Bert started off again. Through the snow he trudged, tossing the white flakes aside with his small but sturdy legs.

All at once, on the white expanse in front of him, Bert saw a movement. At first he thought it was just some loose snow, blown about by the wind, which came in fitful gusts. But as he looked a second time he saw that it was not the wind.

"It's some animal!" exclaimed the boy, speaking aloud, for he wanted company, and, like the men of the desert or wilderness, he fell naturally into the habit of talking to himself. "It's some animal."

Having said this Bert came to a stop, for he knew there might be many sorts of animals in the woods.

"I wonder what it is," he whispered. Somehow or other a whisper seemed more the sort of voice to use in that lonesome place.

A moment later he saw a patch of brown, and then two big ears appeared to be thrust out of a hole in the snow.

"It's a rabbit—a bunny!" cried Bert, and he did not whisper this time.

As he shouted Bert sprang forward through the snow and toward the brown rabbit that had so unexpectedly appeared. Whether it was the boy's shout or his quick movement, or both, was not certain, but the rabbit was frightened and dashed away over the snow, sometimes sinking down almost out of sight, and again, by some means, keeping on the surface of the snow, which was packed harder in some places than in others.

"If I can only get you!" gasped Bert, for his speed through the snow was making him pant and his breath come short. "I'll get you and take you back to Nan and Mrs. Bimby! They won't have enough to eat unless I do, maybe, for it may take me a long while to get back to camp."

Bert had no weapon—he could not even pick up a stone, for they were all covered from sight by the mass of white. But the boy had an idea that he could catch the rabbit alive.

Bert was not a cruel boy, and under other circumstances he never would have dreamed of trying to hurt or catch a bunny. But now he felt that the lives of his sister and Mrs. Bimby might depend on this game.

"I'll get you! I'll run you down!" muttered Bert.

Now a rabbit is a very fast-moving animal. Out West there is a kind called jackrabbits, and they can go faster than the average dog. Only a greyhound or other long-legged dog can beat a jackrabbit running. But though this bunny was not a jackrabbit, being the common wild rabbit of the woods and fields, still it could go faster than could Bert—and in the snow at that.

Every now and again Bert would get so near the bunny that he felt sure that the next moment he would be able to get hold of the long ears. But every time the rabbit would give a desperate jump and get beyond the boy's reach.

"Whew!" exclaimed Bert, as he was forced to stop, because his legs were so tired and because his breath was so short. "I don't wonder hunters have to use guns! They never could get much game just by chasing after it. It wouldn't be any use to set a trap, for I haven't time and I haven't anything to bait it with. Besides, I guess you're so smart you'd never be caught in it."

As Bert came to a stop on top of another little hill where the snow was partly blown away, the rabbit also halted. It looked back at the boy. Probably the bunny was as tired as was Bert.

"If I only had something to throw at you!" murmured the boy. "I can't find any stones, but I can take a stick."

There were trees near at hand, and from the low branches of one of these Bert broke off a number of pieces of dead wood. They cracked like pistol shots, and, turning around to look at the rabbit, Bert saw it scooting away over the snow. Probably the little furry creature thought some hunter was shooting at it.

"Well, I guess I'll have to give up," said the boy, half aloud. "I'll only get lost chasing after you. As it is, I guess I've come 'most a mile out of my way."

He threw the sticks he had broken off, but he did not come anywhere near hitting the brown bunny.

"Oh, well, you're safe! I won't chase you any farther," said Bert. "And I wouldn't have chased you now, and scared you 'most to death, if the folks back in the shack weren't so low on food. Maybe I can find something else."

Bert floundered about in the snow, following his tracks back before they should be filled and so hidden from sight. He was about half way to the place where he had surprised the rabbit when he heard a chattering in a tree over his head.

"A squirrel!" exclaimed the boy. "And a grey one, too, or I miss my guess."

He kept very still, listening. Again, above the noise of the storm was heard the sharp, squealing chatter of a squirrel, and, looking up over his head, Bert saw the animal. It was a large, grey squirrel, with a tail almost as big as its whole body.

The squirrel sat up on a limb and looked down at the boy. It may have been angry or frightened, and it seemed to be scolding Bert as it chattered at him.

Grey squirrels are not such excited scolders as the little red chaps are, but this one did very well.

"If you know what's good for you, you'll go back into your nest and stay there," Bert said. "I can't get you, and you ought to know it, for I haven't a gun and I never could throw up a stick and knock you down. You'd be good eating if I could," Bert went on, for he had often heard his father tell of broiled squirrels.

Bert could see a hole in the tree half way up the trunk, and he guessed that here the squirrel had his winter nest. It would be well lined with dried leaves, soft grass, and perhaps some cotton from the milkweed pods. Thus the squirrels keep warm, wrapping their big bushy tails about them.

"Well, I guess I'll say good-bye to you," went on Bert, as he turned aside from the squirrel in the tree and resumed his trudging through the snow. The weather was cold, and Bert was cold likewise. Also he was tired. His legs ached and his shoulders pained him, for walking through the snow is not easy work, as you who have tried it know.

However, he knew that he must keep bravely on, and so, after turning once or twice, making sure he could not see the cabin, he went along faster.

It was because of his speed that an accident happened to Bert which might have been a very serious one. He was traveling with his head held down, to keep the falling snow out of his face, when he suddenly felt himself falling.

Down, down he went, as though he had stepped into some big hole, or off some high cliff. He gave a cry of alarm, and threw out both hands to grasp something to save himself, but there was nothing to grasp. Down, down went poor Bert!

It was a good thing there was so much snow on the ground. The piles and drifts of white flakes were like so many heaps of feathers, and Bert was thankful when at last, after sliding, slipping, falling and tumbling, he came to a stop, half buried in a deep drift. He was somewhat shaken up, and he had dropped his package of lunch, but at first he did not think he was much hurt until he tried to move his left leg.

Then such a pain shot through the boy that he had to cry aloud. He shut his eyes and leaned back against the pile of snow into which he had fallen. The first flash of pain passed, and he began to feel a little better. But a terrible thought came to him.

"What if my leg is broken?" said Bert, half aloud. "I can't walk, I can't go for help, and I'll have to stay here. Daddy or nobody will know where to find me—not even Nan or Mrs. Bimby! Oh, this is terrible!"

But he knew he must be brave, for he had to help not only himself but his sister and the old woman in the cabin. Clenching his teeth to keep back the cry of pain which he felt would come when he moved his leg again, Bert shifted it a little to one side. The spasm of pain came, but not so bad as at first.

"Maybe it's only broken a little," thought the boy. "And I can crawl, if I can't walk." He had read of hunters and trappers who, with a broken or badly cut leg, had crawled miles over the snow to get help. Bert wanted to be as brave as these heroes.

But when he moved his leg for the third time and found the pain not quite so bad, he began to take heart. He brushed away the snow from both legs and looked at them. They appeared to be all right, but the left one felt a little queer. And it was not until he had managed to pull himself up, by means of a stunted bush showing through the snow, that Bert knew his leg was not broken.

It was strained a little, and it hurt some when he bore his weight on it, but he found that he could at least walk, if he could not run, and he was thankful for this. He looked up toward the place from where he had fallen, and saw that, without knowing it, he had stepped over the edge of a steep hill. The snow had hidden the edge from Bert, and he had plunged right over it.

"Where's my lunch?" he asked aloud, and then he saw the package, which had fallen to one side of the place where he had plunged into the drift. Bert picked it up, and then, thankful that his accident was no worse, he went on again.

"I guess maybe the brook is here," he said, for he noticed that he was down in a valley, and he knew that water always sought low levels. "I'll walk along here," said Bert.

He was so frightened, thinking of what might have happened if he had been crippled and unable to walk, that he did not feel hungry, though it was some time since breakfast. On he trudged through the snow, looking for signs of the brook, which he hoped would lead him to Cedar Camp.

It was while he was passing through a clump of woods that Bert received another fright—one that caused him to run on as fast as he could, in spite of his aching leg.

He had gone half way through the clump of trees, and he was wondering if he would ever come to the brook, when suddenly he heard a noise in a clump of bushes. The noise sounded louder than usual, because it was all so still and quiet near him.

Before Bert could guess what caused the sound, he saw, pushing its way through the underbrush, a tawny animal, with black spots underneath and with little tufts of hair on its ears. At once Bert knew what this was—a wildcat, or lynx!

For a moment Bert was so frightened that he just stood still, looking at the wildcat. And then, as the animal gave a sort of snarl and growl, the boy turned with a yell of fright and ran off through the snow as fast as he could go!

Snowball Bullets

About the time that Bert Bobbsey was running through the snow, to get away from the wildcat, Flossie and Freddie were having a scare of their own, some miles distant from him, though in the same woods around Cedar Camp.

The two smaller Bobbsey twins had gone off without letting their father or mother know, taking with them a lunch. They tramped through the forest until they came to a lonely place and had not yet caught sight of their father, who had started off ahead with Old Jim Bimby and Tom Case. Right here the small twins heard a growl and saw a movement in the bushes.

"What's that?" asked Flossie, shrinking closer to Freddie.

"I–I don't know," Freddie answered, trying to think of something to make him brave. "Maybe it's a bear!"

"A bear?" questioned his sister.

"Yep!" Freddie went on, his eyes never moving from the bush that seemed to hide some animal. "Maybe it's a bear like the one we found the skin of in the attic."

"It–it can't be the *same one* coming back for his skin, can it?" asked Flossie.

"Course not!" declared Freddie. "How could a bear go 'round without his skin on?"

"Well, a bear's skin is just the same to him as our clothes are to us," Flossie went on. "An' sometimes, when we go swimming, we don't have very many clothes on."

"Well, a bear is different," said Freddie.

"Oh, look!" suddenly cried the little girl, and, pointing to the bush with one hand, she clung to Freddie's arm with the other. "He's coming out! He's coming out!" she exclaimed.

A shaggy head could be seen thrusting itself from the bushes, and the children were wondering what sort of animal it could be, for it did not look like a bear, when, with a joyful bark, there burst out in front of them—the shaggy dog belonging to Tom Case!

Rover—Rover was the name of the dog—rushed toward Flossie and Freddie, leaping joyfully and wagging his tail. He had made friends with the children as soon as they came to Cedar Camp, and they loved Rover.

"Oh, hello!" cried Flossie, as if greeting an old friend.

"He's glad to see us and we're glad to see him," said Freddie.

This seemed to be true, though I think Flossie and Freddie were more pleased to see Rover than he was to see them, for the dog knew how to find his way home, and even trace and find his master if need be, while, to tell you the truth, Flossie and Freddie were lost, though they did not yet know it. But they were soon to find this out.

"Did you come looking for us?" asked Flossie, as she patted the shaggy animal.

"I guess he did," Freddie said. "I guess he'd rather come with us than with daddy and the others. Though we'll take Rover to 'em, won't we?"

"Yes," agreed Flossie. "But we must hurry up and catch 'em, Freddie. We want to see Mrs. Bimby and tell her about the nice warm bear robe."

"Sush! Don't speak so loud," cautioned Freddie, looking over his shoulder.

"Why not?" Flossie wanted to know.

"I mean about the bear robe," her brother went on. "There might be some bears in the woods, and if they heard there was the skin of one of 'em at the cabin, maybe they wouldn't like it."

"Maybe that's so," agreed Flossie, also looking around. "But, anyhow, Rover'd drive the bears away; wouldn't you, Rover?"

The dog barked and wagged his tail, which was the only answer he could give. It satisfied the children, and soon they started off again, making their way through the snow, hoping they would soon catch up with their father, Mr. Case and Mr. Bimby. Rover accompanied Flossie and Freddie, sometimes ahead of them and sometimes behind.

The dog had started out, as he often did, to follow his master, but had lagged behind, perhaps to run after a rabbit or squirrel. Then he had come across the tracks of the children and had gone to them, knowing they were friends of his.

"I'm hungry," said Flossie, after a while. "Let's sit under a Christmas tree and eat, Freddie."

"All right," agreed her brother, always willing to do this.

They were, just then, in a clump of evergreen trees, and under some the snow was not as deep as it was in the open. In fact the children found one tree with no snow under it at all, so thick were the branches, and so close to the ground did they come. Crawling into this little nest, where the ground was covered with the dry needles from the pines and other trees, Flossie and Freddie opened the packages of lunch they had brought with them.

Rover, smelling the food, crawled into the shelter after them, and Flossie and Freddie shared their lunch with the dog, who even ate the crumbs off the ground.

"But we mustn't eat everything," said Freddie, when part of the lunch had been disposed of, Rover getting his share.

"Why not?" asked Flossie. "Can't you eat all you want to when you're hungry?"

"It's best to save some," Freddie answered. "Maybe we'll get stuck in the snow and can't get anything more to eat for a while, and then we'll be glad to have this."

"That's so," agreed Flossie, after thinking it over. "I guess I'm not so very hungry. But Rover is. He's terrible hungry, Freddie. See him look at the lunch."

Indeed the dog seemed to be following, with hungry eyes, every motion of the little boy who was wrapping up again that part of the lunch not eaten by him and his sister. They saved about half of it.

Rover sniffed and snuffed as only a dog can, but he made no effort to take the lunch that Freddie placed in a crotch of the evergreen tree which made such a nice shelter for him and his sister.

"Don't you take it, Rover!" cautioned Flossie, shaking her finger at him.

Rover thumped his tail on the ground, perhaps to show that he would be good and mind.

"It's nice and warm in here," Freddie remarked, after a while. "I wish we could stay here longer, Flossie."

"Can't we?"

"Not if we want to go to Mrs. Bimby's," Freddie answered. "We have to get out and walk some more. And it's snowing again, too."

Whether it was or not, the children could not be quite certain, for the wind was blowing, and if the flakes were not falling from the sky they were blowing up off the ground.

It was almost the same, anyhow, for there was a fine shower of the cold, white flakes in the air, and it was much more cosy and warm under the tree than out in the open.

"Let's stay here a little longer," begged Flossie. "Rover likes it here, don't you?" she asked, as she reached out her hand and patted the shaggy back of the dog.

And from the manner in which Rover thumped his tail on the ground you could tell that he did, indeed, like to be with the little Bobbsey twins under the shelter of the tree.

"I know what we can do," said Freddie, after thinking a moment. "I know what we can do to have some fun!"

"What?" asked Flossie, always ready for anything of this sort.

"We'll throw a lot of these pine cones outside, and Rover will chase after 'em and bring 'em back," went on Freddie. "He likes to run out in the snow. And after we play that awhile maybe it will be nicer outside."

"All right," agreed Flossie. "We'll throw pine cones."

There were many of these on the pine-needle covered ground beneath the sheltering tree. The cones were really the clusters of seeds from the tree, and they had become hard and dry so they made excellent things to throw for a dog to bring back.

Rover liked to race after sticks when thrown by the children, and the pine cones were ever so much better than sticks. There were so many of them, too.

"I'll throw first, and then it will be your turn, Flossie," Freddie said. "Here, Rover!" he called to the dog, as he picked up several of the cones.

Always ready for a lark of this sort, Rover leaped to his feet and stood at "attention." Freddie bent aside some of the branches and tossed a pine cone out of the opening.

It fell in a bank of snow some distance away, for Freddie was a good thrower for a little boy. And the pine cone, being light, did not sink down in the snow as a stone would have done.

"Bow-wow!" barked Rover, as he dashed out after the pine cone.

That was his way of saying he would bring it back as quickly as he could. And as Rover rushed from under the little green tent of the pine tree Flossie gave a cry of surprise.

"What's the matter?" asked Freddie, turning around to look at his sister.

"Rover knocked me down!" she answered with a laugh, and, surely enough, there she was sprawling on the brown pine needles which covered the ground under the tree. "He just bunked into me and knocked me over!"

Rover was not used to playing with children, you see, and he was a bit rough. But he didn't mean to be.

Flossie sat up, still laughing, for she was not in the least hurt, and by this time Rover had brought back the pine cone that Freddie had tossed out.

"Good dog, Rover!" cried Freddie, patting the animal as he laid down the cone and wagged his tail. "Now it's your turn to throw one, Flossie," Freddie said.

"All right," Flossie answered. "But look out he doesn't knock you down, Freddie."

"I'm looking out!" Freddie said, and he quickly moved over to one side of the space under the tree, while Flossie threw out her cone.

Flossie was not quite so good a thrower of sticks, stones, or pine cones as was her brother. But she did pretty well. Though her cone did not go as far as Freddie's had, it sank farther down into the snow. Maybe the cone was a heavier one, or it may have fallen in a softer place in the snow. Anyhow it went quite deep into a drift and Rover had to dig with his forepaws to get it so he could take it in his mouth.

"Oh, look at him!" cried Flossie, as the dog, digging away, made the snow fly in a shower back of him. "He's like a snowplow on the railroad!"

Once, in a big storm, Flossie and Freddie had seen the railroad snowplow, pushed by two locomotives, cut through a high drift. And the way Rover scattered the snow made the little girl think of the plow.

"Bring it here, Rover!" cried Freddie, for it would be his turn next to throw a cone.

"Bow-wow!" barked the dog, and then, with a final dive into the drift, he got the brown cone in his mouth and came racing back with it. Covered with snow as he was, he crawled under the shelter to be petted and talked kindly to by Freddie and Flossie.

Then, just as he probably did when he came out of the water in the summer time, Rover gave himself a shake, to get rid of the snowflakes.

"Oh! Oh!" laughed Flossie, holding her hands over her face. "Stop it, Rover! You're getting me all snow!"

But Rover kept it up until he had got off all the snow, and then he raced out again after more cones as the children threw them.

If Bert Bobbsey could have known where his little sister and brother were, with brave old Rover beside them, I am sure he would have wished to join them. For Bert, about this time, was running away from the wildcat that had suddenly burst through the bushes.

"You're not going to get me!" said Bert to himself, as he clutched his package of lunch and raced on as well as he could.

The pain in his leg bothered him, but he was not going to stop for a thing like that and let a wildcat maul him. On he ran through the snow, taking the easiest path he could find. He looked back over his shoulder once or twice, to find the wildcat bounding lightly along after him.

And after he had looked back and had seen the size of the animal and noticed that there was only one, somehow or other Bert became braver, and he had an idea that perhaps he might drive this beast away.

Wildcats, or bobcats as they are sometimes called, being also known as the bay lynx, are not as large as a good-sized dog. They weigh about thirty pounds, and though they have sharp teeth and claws they very seldom attack persons. Only when they are disturbed, or fear that someone is going to harm their little ones or take away their food, do bobcats run after persons.

And this one must have thought Bert was going to do it some harm, for the animal certainly chased the lad.

"Ho!" said Bert to himself, as he looked back, "you're not so big! Maybe you have got sharp teeth and claws, but if you don't get near me you can't hurt me! I'm going to make you go back!"

Bert had a sudden idea of how he might do this—with snowball bullets. All about him was snow—piles of it—and Bert had often taken part in snowball fights at home. He was a good thrower, and once he had snowballed a savage dog that had run at Flossie and Freddie and had caused the animal to run yelping away.

"I'm going to snowball this wildcat!" decided Bert.

He ran on a little farther until he came to a small clearing where the trees stood in an irregular ring around an open place. There Bert decided to make a stand and see if he could not drive the chasing wildcat away.

"And if he won't go, and comes after me," thought Bert, "I can climb a tree."

He did not know, or else had forgotten, that wildcats themselves are very good tree-climbers.

Reaching the other side of the clearing, Bert laid his package of lunch down on a firm place in the snow, and then rapidly began to make some hard, round balls. He packed them with all his might between his mittened hands, for he knew a soft snowball would not be of much use against a wildcat.

He had been some distance ahead of the animal, and when it ran up to the edge of the clearing Bert had several snowballs ready.

"Come on now! See how you like that!" cried the boy. He threw one snowball "bullet," but he was so excited that it went high over the head of the bobcat. The next one struck in the snow at the feet of the animal. But the third one hit it right on the nose!

"Good shot!" cried Bert.

The wildcat uttered a snarl and a growl, and stopped for a moment. Perhaps it had never before chased anyone who threw snowballs.

"Have another!" cried Bert, and the next white bullet struck it on the side. The bobcat leaped up in the air, and then Bert threw another ball which hit it on the head.

This was too much for the creature. With a loud howl it turned and ran back into the woods, and Bert breathed easier.

"Well, I guess as long as I can throw snowballs you won't get me," he said to himself, as he picked up the package of lunch and hurried on.

On the Rock

Bert Bobbsey felt very proud of himself after he had driven away the wildcat with snowballs. And I think he had a right to be proud. Not many boys of his age would have dared to stand and await the oncoming of a beast that is quite dangerous once it starts to claw and bite. But Bert had spent so much time in the woods and out in the open that he was very self-reliant.

And so, after looking back once or twice as he left the clearing, and finding that the bobcat did not follow, Bert began to feel much better.

"I'll soon be at Cedar Camp," he said to himself, "and then I'll be all right. I'll send 'em back to get Nan and take something to eat to Mrs. Bimby. I'll be glad to see Flossie and Freddie again."

Had Bert only known it, Flossie and Freddie were nearer to him than if they had been in Cedar Camp, though the small Bobbsey twins were still some distance from their brother.

And while Mr. Bobbsey was forging ahead through the snow with Old Jim Bimby and Tom Case, knowing nothing, of course, about his little boy and girl having followed him, Mrs. Bobbsey was having worries of her own about the absence of the small children from the cabin.

She and Mrs. Baxter had missed Flossie and Freddie soon after the men had started on the searching trip, but, for a time, the mother of the two small twins was not at all worried. She thought Flossie and Freddie had merely run out to play a little, as it was the first chance they had had since the big storm began.

But when, after a while, they had not come back to the cabin, and she could see nothing of them, Mrs. Bobbsey said:

"Mrs. Baxter, have you seen Flossie and Freddie?"

"No, Mrs. Bobbsey, I haven't," answered the cook. "But it looks as if they had been in the pantry, for things there are all upset."

Mrs. Bobbsey looked around the kitchen and pantry, and she at once guessed part of what had happened.

"They've packed up lunch for themselves," she said to the housekeeper, "and they've gone out to play. Well, they'll be all right as long as they stay around here and it doesn't storm again. I'll go and look for them in a few minutes."

But when she did look and call Flossie and Freddie, they were not to be found. Indeed, they were more than a mile away by this time, and they had just met Rover, as I have told you.

"I'm glad Rover's with us, aren't you, Freddie?" asked Flossie, as they made ready to set off again, after having eaten their lunch.

"Lots glad," answered the little boy. "Mrs. Bimby will be glad to see him, I guess."

Indeed Mrs. Bimby, left alone with Nan after Bert had gone out, would have been glad to see almost anyone. For she was worried because her husband was away and because there was so little left in the house to eat, only she did not want to tell Nan so. And she did not think she could shoot another rabbit, as Bert had done.

"I do hope that boy will find my Jim or someone and bring help," thought Mrs. Bimby.

And of course Mr. Bobbsey with Old Jim and Tom Case were on their way to the cabin, but they had to go slowly on account of so much snow.

The snow was worse for Flossie and Freddie than for any of the others in the woods, because the legs of the small twins were so short. It was hard work for them to wade through the drifts. But they felt a little better after their rest under the "Christmas tree," as Flossie called it, and after they had eaten some of their lunch. So on they trudged again.

"Maybe we can find daddy's lost Christmas trees," suggested Freddie, after a while.

"Wouldn't he be glad if we did?" cried Flossie. "Here, Rover! Come back!" she called, for the dog was running too far ahead to please her and Freddie.

The dog came racing back, scattering the snow about as he plunged through it, and Flossie patted his shaggy head.

"Don't you think we'll find daddy pretty soon?" asked Flossie, after she and Freddie had trudged on for perhaps half an hour longer. "I'm getting tired in my legs."

"So'm I," her brother admitted. "I wish we could find 'em. But if we don't, pretty soon, we'll go back, 'cause I think it's going to snow some more."

Indeed, the sky seemed to be getting darker behind the veil of snow clouds that hung over it, and some swirling flakes of white began sifting down.

Freddie came to a stop and looked about him. He was tired, and so was Flossie. The only one of the party who seemed to enjoy racing about in the drifts was Rover. He never appeared to get tired.

"I guess maybe we'd better go back," said Freddie, after thinking it over. "We haven't much left to eat, and I guess daddy can tell Mrs. Bimby about the bear skin to keep her warm."

"I guess so," agreed Flossie. "It's going to be night pretty soon."

It would be some hours until night, however, and the darkness was caused by gathering storm clouds, but Flossie and Freddie did not know that. They turned about, and began to go back along the way they had come. At least they thought they were doing that, but they had not gone far before Flossie said:

"Freddie, we've come the wrong way."

"How do you know?" he asked.

"'Cause we aren't stepping in our own tracks like we would be if we went back straight."

Freddie looked at the snow. It was true. There was no sign of the tracks they must have made in walking along. Before this they had known which way they were going. Now they didn't.

"We—we're lost!" faltered Flossie.

"Oh, maybe not," said Freddie as cheerfully as he could. But still, when he realized that they had not walked along their back track, he knew they must be going farther into the woods, or at least away from Cedar Camp.

"Oh, I don't like to be lost!" wailed Flossie. "I want to go home!"

Freddie did too, but he hoped he wouldn't cry about it. Boys must be brave and not cry, he thought.

But as the little Bobbsey twins stood there, not knowing what to do, it suddenly became colder, the wind sprang up, and down came a blinding storm of snow, so thick that they could not see Rover, who, a moment before, had been tumbling about in the drifts near them.

"Oh! Oh!" cried Flossie. "Let's go home, Freddie!"

But where was "home" or camp? How were they to get there?

And so, soon after Bert had driven off the wildcat and had run on, this Bobbsey lad, too, was caught in the same snow storm that had frightened Flossie and Freddie. But of course Bert did not know that.

"Say, we've had enough snow for a winter and a half already," thought Bert, as he saw more white flakes coming down. "And it isn't Christmas yet! I hope I'm not going to be snowed in out here all alone! I'd better hurry!"

As Bert trudged along through the storm he found himself becoming thirsty. If you have ever walked a long distance, even in a snowstorm, you may have felt the same way yourself. And perhaps you have tried to quench your thirst and cool your mouth by eating snow. If you have, you doubtless remember that instead of getting less thirsty you were only made more so. This is what always happens when a person eats snow. Ice is different, if you hold pieces of it in your mouth until it melts.

"My! I wish I had a drink," exclaimed Bert, speaking aloud, as he had done a number of times since setting out alone to bring help to Nan and Mrs. Bimby. "I wish I had a drink of water!"

Now Bert Bobbsey knew better than to eat dry snow. Once when he was a small boy, smaller even than Freddie, he had been playing out in the snow and had eaten it whenever he felt thirsty. As a result he had been made ill.

"Never eat snow again, Bert," his father had told him at the time. And to make Bert remember Mr. Bobbsey had read the boy a story of travelers in the Arctic regions searching for the North Pole. The story told how, no matter how tired or cold these travelers were, they always stopped to melt the snow and make water or tea of it when they were thirsty. They never ate dry snow.

"I've either got to find a spring to get a drink, or melt some of this snow," said Bert to himself, as he walked on, limping a little, though his leg was feeling better than at first. "But I guess if I did find a spring it would be frozen over. Now how can I melt some snow?"

Bert had been on camping trips with his father, and he had often seen Mr. Bobbsey make use of things he found beside the road or in the woods to help out in a time of some little trouble. With this in mind, the boy began to look around for something that would help him get a drink of water, or to melt some snow into water which he could drink after it had cooled.

But to melt snow needed a fire, he knew, and also something that would hold the snow before and after it was melted.

"I need a pan or a can and a fire," decided Bert. "I wonder if I have any matches?"

He felt in his pockets and found some, though he did not usually carry them, for they are rather dangerous for children. But Bert felt that he was now getting to be quite a boy.

"Well, here's a start," he said to himself as he felt the matches in his pocket. But he did not take them out, for the snow was blowing about, and Bert knew that a wet match was as bad as none at all. He must keep his matches dry as the old settlers were advised to "keep their powder dry."

"If I could only make a fire," thought Bert, coming to a stop and looking about him at a spot that looked as if it might once have been a camp. All he could see was a waste of snow and some trees. But wood for fires, he knew, grew on trees, though any wood which could be made to burn must be dry.

"Maybe I could scrape away some snow and make a fire," thought Bert. "The thing I need most, though, is a tin can to hold snow and water. Ouch! My leg hurts!" he exclaimed.

His leg, just then, seemed to get a "kink" in it, as he said afterward. He kicked out, as football players do sometimes when their legs get twisted.

As it happened, Bert kicked his foot into a little pile of snow, and next he was surprised to find that he had kicked something out. At first it seemed to be a lump of ice, but as it rolled a few feet and the snow fell away, the boy found that he had kicked into view an empty tin tomato can!

"Here's luck!" cried Bert, as he sprang after the can before it could be covered from sight in the snow again. "This sure is luck! I can melt some snow in this now!"

Taking the can in his hand he knocked it against his shoe, thus getting rid of the snow that filled it. The can was opened half way, and the tin top was bent back, making a sort of handle to it, which Bert was glad to see. It would enable him without burning his fingers to lift the can off the fire he intended to build.

"All I need now is some dry wood, and I can make a fire and melt snow to make water," he said aloud. "If I had some tea I could make a regular hot drink, like they have up at the North Pole. But I guess water will be all right. Now for some wood!"

He made his way over to a clump of trees and, by kicking away the snow, he managed to find some dead sticks. As the snow was dry they were not very wet, but Bert feared they were not dry enough to kindle quickly. And he had only a few matches.

"I've got some paper, though," he told himself, as lie felt in his pockets. "A little soft, dry wood, and that, will start a fire and the other wood will burn, even if it is a little damp."

One of the lessons Bert's father had taught him was to make a campfire, and Bert put some of this instruction to use now. He hunted about until he found a fallen log, and by clearing away the snow at one end he revealed a rotten end. This soft wood made very good tinder, to start a fire.

The outer end of the rotten log was rather damp. But by kicking away this latter, Bert got at some wood that was quite dry—just what he wanted.

He swung his foot that was not lame from side to side, clearing a place on the ground at one side of the log, and there he laid his paper and the wood to start his fire.

You may be sure Bert was very anxious as he struck one of his few matches and held it to the paper. He hardly breathed as he watched the tiny flame. And then, all at once, the blaze flickered out after it had caught one edge of the paper!

"This is bad luck!" murmured Bert. "I've got a few more chances, though."

He crumpled up the paper in a different shape, arranged it carefully under the pile of splinters and rotten wood, and struck another match. This time he made sure to hold in his breath completely, for it was his breath before, he feared, that had blown out the match.

This time the paper caught and blazed up merrily. Bert wanted to shout and cry "hurrah!" but he did not. The fire was not really going yet, and he was getting more and more thirsty all the while. It was all he could do not to scoop up some of the dry snow and cram it into his mouth. But he held back.

"I'll have some water melted in a little while," he told himself. "My fire is going now."

And, indeed, the tiny flame had caught the soft wood and was beginning to ignite the twigs. From them the larger and heavier pieces of wood would catch, and then he could set the can of snow on to melt into water.

Still hardly daring to breathe, Bert fed his fire in the shelter of the half snow-covered log. It was beginning to melt the snow all around it now, but of course this melted snow ran away and was lost. Bert could not drink that.

When the fire was going well, Bert kicked around on the ground under the log until he found some stones. With these he made a little fireplace, enclosing the blaze, and when he had some embers there, with more wood at hand to pile on, he brought the can to the fire and scooped the tin full of snow.

"This is going to be my teakettle," said Bert, with a little smile. "Mother and Nan would laugh if they could see me now."

If you have ever melted a pan of snow on even so good a fire as is in your mother's kitchen range, you know that snow melts very slowly. It was this way with Bert. He thought the snow in the can would never melt down into water, and when it did, and was fairly boiling, he took hold of the top and threw all the water out!

Why did he do that? you ask. Well, because he wanted to be sure the can was clean, and his mother had told him that boiling water would destroy almost any kind of germ. The can might have had germs in it, having lain outdoors a long time.

"But now I guess it's clean," Bert said, as he again filled it with snow after he had rinsed it out. Then he waited for the second quantity of snow to melt, and when this had cooled, which did not take very long, Bert took a drink. The snow water did not taste very good—boiled water very seldom does—but it was safer than eating dry snow.

"Well, now I must travel on," said Bert, as he scattered snow over the fire to put it out. "I'll carry a little water with me in the can, for I may get thirsty again. It won't freeze for a while."

He walked along as fast as he could, with the pain in his leg, but the snow came down harder and faster and the wind blew colder. Bert looked about for some place of shelter and saw where one tree had blown over against another, making a sort of little den, or cave, near the side of a high rock, which was so steep that the snow had not clung to it, leaving the big stone bare.

"I'll go in there and stay awhile," thought Bert, as he caught sight of this shelter. "Maybe the storm won't last long."

But as he started to enter the place he heard a growl! There was a scurrying in the dried leaves that formed a carpet for the den, and then, in the half-darkness, Bert saw two green eyes staring at him! He smelled a wild odor, too, that told him some beast of the forest dwelt in this den.

"Oh! A wildcat!" cried Bert, as, a moment later, there sprang out at him the same animal, or one very like it, that he had snowballed a little while before. Probably it was another lynx, but Bert did not stop to think of this.

Forgetting his plan of using snowball bullets, Bert dropped his little bundle of lunch, part of which he had eaten, and began to climb the nearest tree.

He learned then, if he did not know it before, that a wildcat, which was the animal he had surprised in its den, is a good tree-climber; as good as your house cat, or even better.

When half way up the tree, Bert looked down and saw the yellow wildcat coming after him. Probably the animal thought that Bert had no right near its den.

"This is bad!" thought Bert, as he climbed higher and higher. Then, as he saw the beast still coming, he realized that he must, somehow, get away. He saw the big rock not far from the tree. The rock had a small flat top, covered with snow, but the sides were smooth and almost straight up and down, and had no snow on them.

"If I could get there the wildcat couldn't get me," thought Bert. "And if it tries to jump after me I can snowball it. I'm going to get on the rock!"

It was the best plan he could think of, and a moment later, having got in good position, he gave a jump, left the tree, and landed in the soft snow on top of the big rock.

With a snarl and a growl the wildcat stopped climbing up as it saw what the boy had done. Then it began climbing down the tree while Bert, from his place of safety, watched. He wondered what the bobcat would do.

The animal walked over to where Bert had dropped his package of lunch and began tearing at the paper.

"Maybe if he eats that he won't want to get me," thought Bert. "But how long shall I have to stay here?"

The wildcat, having eaten Bert's lunch, which did not take long, looked up at the boy on the rock. It sniffed at the base of the big stone, and reared up with its forepaws against it.

"You can't climb here!" called Bert aloud. "If you do I'll hit you on the nose with snowballs!"

And then, as though to add to the boy's troubles, it began to snow hard, a wall of white flakes falling around the lone laddie on the big rock.

Found at Last

Bert Bobbsey was really frightened and alarmed, caught as he was in the storm on the big rock, with a wildcat sniffing around at the bottom. He could not even see well enough to throw snowballs at the creature, and, even if he could have driven it away, he felt that it would not be safe for him to come down off the big stone.

"He can't get me while I'm up here, I don't believe," said Bert to himself. "But I can't stay here very long, or I'll be snowed under. What shall I do?"

Indeed he was in what he said afterward was a "regular pickle." And then Bert thought of calling for help. He wondered why he had not done that before.

Standing up on the high rock Bert sent his voice shouting out into the storm.

"Help! Help! Help!" he shouted.

Bert did not know just whom he expected to help him. He did not know how far he was from Mrs. Bimby's cabin, nor how far he was away from Cedar Camp. All he knew was that he was in trouble and needed help. The only way was to shout as loudly as he could.

At his first call the wildcat at the foot of the rock snarled, growled, and tried to leap up. But the sides were too steep and smooth. Bert could catch glimpses of the animal when the snow came down a little less heavily now and again, making a sort of opening in the white curtain.

"Help! Help! Help!" cried Bert again and again.

Curiously enough it was Flossie and Freddie, who in the blizzard had wandered near to the rock, who heard Bert's cry. Through the storm the voice came to them, though of course they did not know it was their brother calling.

"Hark!" exclaimed Freddie, who, with his sister, had been floundering about in the drifts, the small Bobbsey twins trying to find their former tracks in the snow so they could work their way back. But the flakes had fallen into their footprints, and had been blown over them so deeply that the prints were blotted out.

"Do you hear that?" asked Freddie of Flossie.

"Yes," she answered, as the voice came to her ears. "It's somebody saying he'll help us."

That is what she thought it was—someone wanting to help her and Freddie, not someone in need of help.

Again came the call, and it sounded so close that the two small Bobbsey twins knew which way to go to reach it.

"We're coming! We're coming!" shouted Freddie. "Come on, Rover! I guess that's daddy coming to help us! We're coming!"

With a bark the dog bounded through the storm after the two children, and you can imagine how surprised Bert Bobbsey on the rock was when he heard shouts in answer to his own. He did not know, of course, that Freddie and Flossie were anywhere near him. He thought it was his father and some of the men from Cedar Camp.

A little later the small Bobbsey twins came within sight of the big rock. They could not see Bert on it on account of the blinding snow. But Rover caught the smell of the wildcat, and with a savage bark he sprang to drive the creature away.

"Good old Rover! Good dog!" cried Bert, as the snow stopped for a moment and he caught sight of the dog that he knew. "Sic him, Rover!"

And Rover rushed at the wildcat with such fierceness that the beast scuttled back to its den under the half-fallen tree. And then Bert looked and saw Flossie and Freddie.

At the same time the small Bobbsey twins looked up and caught a glimpse of their brother on the rock.

"Oh, Bert!" cried Freddie, "did you come out to look for us? We're lost!"

"So am I, I guess," Bert answered, as he jumped down, landing in a bank of soft snow and beginning to pet Rover. "Where in the world did you children come from?"

"We came out after daddy and Mr. Jim and Mr. Case," Freddie went on. "They're going to take some things to Mrs. Bimby."

"Mrs. Bimby!" cried Bert "Why, I left her and Nan this morning. They haven't got hardly anything left to eat. But where is the camp?"

"Don't you know?" asked Freddie. "We don't know. We're lost."

"That's bad," said Bert, looking at the swirling snow all about. "And the wildcat ate my lunch."

"We've a little left," Flossie said. "Did you save any chestnuts, Bert?"

"I brought some, but I ate 'em. But Nan's got some, back at Mrs. Bimby's cabin, if we can find it. You say daddy started out after us?"

"Yes, to find you and Nan and take something to Mrs. Bimby," explained Freddie. "Her husband was at our camp. He got lost in the snow, and he said his wife didn't have anything in the cupboard."

"She didn't—not very much," Bert said. "I shot a rabbit, but I guess that's all eaten now. But say, you two oughtn't to be out here alone!"

"We're not alone now," Flossie said. "We got you with us!"

"Well, I'm glad you met me," Bert said. "And I'm glad Rover drove that wildcat away. I scared one with snowballs, but I couldn't hit this one very well. Now we'd better try to get back to camp. I guess there's going to be another storm."

"Will it snow a whole lot and cover us all up?" asked Flossie, anxiously.

The poor little girl had had quite enough of snow, cold wind, blizzards, and bad weather of all sorts.

"Oh, I guess maybe it won't snow so very hard," answered Bert. He did not want to confess to Flossie and Freddie that he was a bit frightened.

"Maybe Rover could show us which way to go to find Cedar Camp," suggested Freddie. "Dogs are smart, and Rover is a good dog."

"He was nice to us when we sat under the pine tree," went on Flossie. "And he ran out and brought in pine cones and he shook himself and made snow fly all over me."

"You didn't try to eat pine cones, did you?" asked Bert.

"Oh, no," Flossie answered. "We just threw them for Rover to play with. But I'm too tired to play now. I want to go to bed."

"Oh, Flossie, you don't want to go to bed now, do you?" asked Bert. "Why, if you were to lie down in the snow you'd freeze."

"I don't want to go to sleep in the snow," Flossie said, and she was beginning to whine a little. No wonder, for it had been a hard day for her and Freddie.

"No, I don't want to sleep in the snow," the little girl said. "I want my own little bunk at the camp."

"Well, we'll be there pretty soon," Bert said, as kindly as he could.

"Carry me!" begged Flossie, when she had stumbled on a little farther, walking between her two brothers.

"All right. I guess I can carry you," said Bert, but he was worrying about his leg a little. It was not so bad when he bore his own weight on it. But could he carry Flossie?

However, he was not going to give up without trying, and so, when they came to a little sheltered place, where the snow was not quite so deep, Bert stooped down.

"I'll take you pickaback, Flossie," he said.

"Oh, I like that!" laughed his sister, as she climbed up on her brother's back.

Bert was not sure whether or not he was going to like it, but he said nothing. He had to shut his teeth tight to keep from crying out with pain as he straightened up with Flossie on his back, for her weight, small as she was, put too much weight on his injured leg. Flossie was quite "chunky" for her size, as Dinah was wont to say.

"Hold steady now, Flossie," directed Bert, as he straightened up. "Put your arms around my neck."

"I guess I know how to ride piggy-back!" laughed Flossie. She was not so tired now, when something like this happened to change her thoughts.

Bert staggered along through the snow with his sister on his back. Though he did not want to say so, his leg hurt him very much. But he tried not to limp, though Freddie at last noticed it, and asked:

"Have you got a stone in your shoe, Bert?"

"Oh, no, I—I just sprained it a little," Bert answered in a low voice, so Flossie would not hear. For of course if she had known it hurt her brother to carry her she would not ask him to. But just then Flossie was reaching up to take hold of a branch of a tree as Bert passed beneath it. And, catching hold of it, Flossie, with a merry laugh, showered herself and Bert with snow that clung to the branch.

"Don't, Flossie, dear!" Bert had to say. "There's snow enough without pulling down any more. And we'll get plenty if the clouds spill more flakes."

"Do you think it will storm some more?" Freddie wanted to know.

Bert did not answer right away. He was thinking what he could do about Flossie. If she could not walk then she must be carried, but he felt that he could not hold her on his back much longer, his leg was paining too much.

Just then the sight of Rover, the big, strong dog, floundering about in the snow, gave Bert an idea. Rover did not seem to care how much breath or strength he wasted, for he ran everywhere, barking and trying to dig things out from under the drifts.

"Oh, Flossie! wouldn't you like to ride on Rover's back?" asked poor, tired Bert.

"Oh, that will be lovely!" cried the little girl.

"Here, Rover!" cried Freddie.

The dog came leaping through the snow, very likely hoping to have some sticks thrown that he might race after them. But he did not seem surprised when Flossie was placed on his back and held there by Freddie on one side and Bert on the other.

"Now I'm having a ride on a make-believe elephant!" laughed Flossie. Rover could not run with the little girl on his back, and I must say he behaved very nicely, carrying her along through the drifts. Her legs hung "dangling down-o," but that did not matter.

"I guess I'm rested now," said Flossie, after a bit. "I'm cold, and it will make me warmer to walk. I'll walk and hold your hand, Bert."

If Rover was glad to have the load taken from his back he did not say so, but by the way he raced on ahead when Flossie got off I think he was.

"I guess there's more snow coming," suddenly cried Bert.

There was, the flakes coming down almost as thick and fast as when the blizzard first swirled about Cedar Camp. Bert took the hands of Flossie and Freddie and led them on through the storm. It was hard work, and the smaller children were crying with the cold and from fear at the coming darkness when Rover suddenly barked.

"Hark!" cried Bert. "I guess someone is coming!"

"Maybe it's daddy!" half sobbed Flossie.

Shouts were coming through the storm—the shouts of men. Rover barked louder and rushed forward. Bert held to the hands of his brother and sister and peered anxiously through the falling flakes and the fast-gathering darkness.

Suddenly a man rushed forward, and, a moment later, had Flossie and Freddie in his arms, hugging and kissing them. Then he clasped Bert around the shoulders.

"Daddy! Daddy!" cried Flossie and Freddie together. "You found us, didn't you?"

"Yes. But I didn't know you were away from camp," said Mr. Bobbsey, for it was he. "Where's Nan?" he asked Bert quickly, while Rover leaped about his master, Mr. Case, and Old Jim.

"She's at Mrs. Bimby's cabin," Bert answered.

"My wife!" exclaimed Old Jim. "Is she—is she all right?"

"She was when I came away this morning to get help," said Bert. "I shot a rabbit for her and Nan. It was good, too. But I guess she'll need food now."

"We have a lot for her," said Tom Case. "Rover, you rascal!" he went on, patting his dog, "I wondered where you ran away to, but it's a good thing you found the children."

"And he drove away the wildcat," Bert announced.

It was a happy, joyful party in spite of the storm, which was getting worse. Mr. Bobbsey and the two men with him had gotten off the road that led to Old Jim's cabin, and it was because of that fact that they had found the lost children.

"What had we better do?" asked Mr. Bobbsey, when it was learned that Bert, Freddie and Flossie had really suffered no harm from being lost. "Should we go back to Cedar Camp or to your cabin, Mr. Bimby?"

"The cabin is nearer," said Tom Case. "If you folks go there, with Jim to guide you, I'll back track to Cedar Camp and fetch a sled. You can ride the Bobbsey twins home in that."

"Yes, we'd better go to my cabin," said Old Jim. "We can make room for you, and we'll take the food with us."

So this plan was decided on, Tom Case and Rover going to Cedar Camp for the sled, while Mr. Bobbsey, Mr. Bimby and the three children trudged back to Mrs. Bimby's cabin.

You can imagine how glad Nan and the old woman were to see not only Bert but the others.

"Oh, I was afraid when it began to storm again," said Nan, as she hugged Flossie and Freddie. "But I never dreamed you two would be out in it."

"Nor I," said their father.

"You ought to see the bear skin we found!" exclaimed Freddie, to change the subject. "It's going to be for Mrs. Bimby, to keep her warm."

"Bless their hearts!" murmured Old Jim's wife. "I can keep warm all right, but it's hard to get food in a storm."

However, there was plenty of that now, and they all soon gathered about the table and had a hot meal. The second storm was not as bad as the first had been, and later that evening up came a big sled, filled with straw and drawn by powerful horses, and in it was Mrs. Bobbsey and some of the men from Cedar Camp.

After a joyful reunion, in piled the Bobbsey twins with their father and mother, and good-byes were called to the Bimby family, who now had food enough to last through many storms.

There was not much trouble getting to Cedar Camp, though the road was so blocked with snow that once the sled almost upset. But before midnight the Bobbsey twins were back in the cabin, all safe together once again.

"We've had a lot of adventures since we came here," said Bert, as they sat about the cozy fire.

"Too many," remarked his mother. "I don't know when I've been so worried, and it was worse after Flossie and Freddie went away."

"We won't run away again," promised the small twins.

"Did you find your Christmas trees, Daddy?" asked Nan.

"No, not yet," he replied. "I guess they're lost, and we'll have to cut more."

But the next day, when the storm ceased and the sun shone, a man came to camp with word about the missing trees. The railroad cars on which they were loaded had been switched off on a wrong track and had been held at a distant station awaiting someone to claim them. This Mr. Bobbsey did, and soon the shipment of Christmas trees was on its way to Lakeport.

"And as long as they are found there is no excuse for staying in Cedar Camp any longer," said Mr. Bobbsey.

But the children like it so that they prevailed on their father and mother to remain a few days longer. And then the Bobbsey twins had many good times, playing in the woods and about the sawmill. For there came a thaw after the big storms, and most of the snow melted. Bert and Nan got more chestnuts, too.

"But I hope we'll have some snow for Christmas," said Nan.

"So we can make a snow fort!" added Freddie.

"And a snowman and knock his hat off!" laughed Flossie.

"I should think you'd had enough snow," remarked their mother.

But the Bobbsey twins seldom had enough of anything when there was fun and excitement going, and you may be sure this was not the last of their adventures. But now let us say good-bye.

THE END

CPSIA information can be obtained at www.ICGtesting.com
Printed in the USA
BVOW08s0823041013

332803BV00003B/611/P